DIRK LEANED CLOSER . . .

"Now that I've met your brothers, I can see why you're such a good fighter," Dirk said.

Without thinking, Valerie retorted, "That's *not* my only asset." Then she realized what she'd said.

Dirk looked at her figure, outlined by cut-off jeans and a T-shirt. "I'll say." He continued to tease. "What are our chances of getting through the next council meeting without an argument?"

Valerie tried to cover her confusion. "What's on the agenda?"

He laughed. "You certainly are cautious."

Neither of them spoke for a few minutes, but his arm lay across the back of the swing, and Val was conscious of his fingers touching her hair . . .

Bestsellers from SIGNET VISTA

Magic Moments
1

The Love Vote

Jo Stewart

A SIGNET VISTA BOOK

NEW AMERICAN LIBRARY

PUBLISHED BY
THE NEW AMERICAN LIBRARY
OF CANADA LIMITED

PUBLISHER'S NOTE

This novel is a work of fiction. Names, characters, places, and incidents either are the product of the author's imagination or are used fictitiously, and any resemblance to actual persons, living or dead, events, or locales is entirely coincidental.

NAL BOOKS ARE AVAILABLE AT QUANTITY DISCOUNTS WHEN USED TO PROMOTE PRODUCTS OR SERVICES. FOR INFORMATION PLEASE WRITE TO PREMIUM MARKETING DIVISION, NEW AMERICAN LIBRARY, 1633 BROADWAY, NEW YORK, NEW YORK 10019.

Magic Moments™ is a trademark of New American Library

First Printing, June, 1984

2 3 4 5 6 7 8 9

SIGNET VISTA TRADEMARK REG. U.S. PAT. OFF. AND FOREIGN COUNTRIES REGISTERED TRADEMARK — MARCA REGISTRADA HECHO EN WINNIPEG, CANADA

SIGNET, SIGNET CLASSIC, MENTOR, PLUME, MERIDIAN and NAL BOOKS are published in Canada by The New American Library of Canada, Limited, Scarborough, Ontario

PRINTED IN CANADA

COVER PRINTED IN U.S.A.

To
Michelle Tafoya and Ralph Ranalli, Jr.,
school and sports experts

Chapter One

As soon as he introduced himself, Valerie Robinson knew Dirk Atwood spelled trouble. Leadership camp was supposed to teach student body officers to take command, but his authoritative manner and compelling voice would daunt a five-star general.

Although the California sun slanting through the university windows attractively reddened Dirk's brown hair and lightened his dark eyes, Val was on her guard. One look at his strong jaw and stubborn mouth told her she'd be in for a tough year.

"Is that him?" Nell squinted, pushing her tumbled blonde hair from a face whose dimples had caused more than one athlete to break training.

"Why don't you wear your contacts?" Val demanded, tired of playing Seeing Eye dog.

"I forgot."

That was not entirely true, for Val knew Nell avoided wearing them whenever possible. She claimed they bothered her. Val suspected Nell had read somewhere that nearsighted people should exercise their eyes to improve them. Nell was a sucker for natural cures.

"So tell me," she nudged Val now. "Is it him or not?"

Val eyed the commanding figure warily. "I'm afraid so."

Nell had no such fears. "Don't worry. We can handle him."

Val envied Nell's confidence as well as her effect on guys. Even now the quarterback sitting next to her was inching closer. The irony was that Nell preferred Val's looks to her own California blondeness.

"What I wouldn't give for black hair," she often sighed, fingering the tip of Val's hair which just brushed her shoulders. "Mine's hopeless. I could never get it to hang straight. You look like Cleopatra," she decided. "Remember Liz Taylor in that?" They had watched the old movie on television. "You even have her eyes!"

This wasn't quite true, as Val's eyes were light blue not violet, but then Nell was prejudiced. She'd been Val's best friend since sixth grade. Not long after that, Val's dad had labeled them the twin terrors when they'd conned her brothers into trying their soap-filled brownies.

But at seventeen they were no longer children, and what Val didn't like to admit was the strange sensation in the pit of her stomach when she looked at Dirk. Nor did she like the way he avoided mentioning her in his speech. After all, she was going to be his co-president.

Winding up his goals as student body president, he concluded, "I intend to work for better communication between our student body officers and the administration . . ."

He did, did he? And what would she be doing? Polishing his gavel? Val's temper was beginning to rise.

" . . . and what I most want to accomplish

as president is having everyone pull his own weight."

"Admirable," observed the leadership counselor who was in charge of the seminar. "But that would mean getting the cooperation of everyone involved. Won't that present any problems?" His voice was lightly satiric.

It sure would if he continued to deny her existence, Val fumed.

"No, nothing I can't handle."

That did it! "Can you handle the problem of joining two rival campuses?" she challenged.

The counselor swiveled so fast his glasses flew from his nose. "And you are?"

"Valerie Robinson, co-president with Dirk," she announced.

Val knew by his grim expression that Dirk didn't appreciate her interruption, but she'd had just about enough of hearing what *he* intended. Whatever happened to *we*?

The counselor retrieved his glasses and anchored them more firmly. "One would expect that as co-presidents, you would already be acquainted."

"No," Nell broke in. "Val and I come from the other campus, Winona High."

"Nell is co-commissioner of entertainment with Tim Merrick from Miramar," Val explained, as heads craned to get a better look at her blonde friend. "We'd all been elected before . . ." She still found the words difficult to say. "Before the school board closed us down."

The bitterness was there, although Val tried to follow her father's advice: "Mourn now for losing your school. You should. It's like having someone you love die. But when you go to Miramar in the fall, be ready to move forward. Don't fight them."

Looking at Dirk, who represented the Miramar students, she wondered if that would be possible.

But he surprised her. "Sorry we didn't get to meet sooner." His grin was rueful. "Probably would have stopped me from shooting off my mouth."

The kids liked the way he freely admitted he was wrong, and even Val felt the pull of his personality.

But before she could respond, the counselor took over. "Usually, I ask each officer to come up with three adjectives describing him or herself." He looked at Dirk. "Perhaps you'd like to start?"

"After what just happened," Dirk admitted, "I'd have to say cocky, conceited, and stupid."

The kids laughed as the counselor motioned to Val, who could feel her face getting red.

By being so candid, Dirk had put her on the spot. "Determined, impulsive, and . . . quick-tempered." She sat down to a good-natured round of applause.

"And I'd have to add a sense of humor to both your lists," the counselor said approvingly. He looked around. "Now, what about the rest of you?"

During the remainder of the morning, other school officers came forward to introduce themselves. When it was nearly noon, the counselor took over once more.

"I must compliment you. I don't remember when I've seen a more qualified group, and I know you're going to make the most of your week at Santa Theresa University." He rubbed a hand through his bushy hair. "As you know, this is the first of three sessions run by the California Association of Student Councils. We want you to feel relaxed enough to participate and enjoy all the programs we've planned."

He leaned forward, lightly balancing on the balls of his feet. "Now, as you heard at orientation, your mornings will be devoted to seminars, ranging from how to organize your time to how to run a good pep rally."

The noon bell from the clock tower interrupted, and he shrugged. "Time to let you sample the gourmet delights awaiting you at the university cafeteria."

"You've got to be kidding!"

"My dog gets better food!"

"I see you've already become acquainted with the cuisine." He leaned forward again, a conspiratorial grin on his lean face. "To avoid starvation, might I suggest you follow the lead of your counselors." He then proceeded to list for them all the nearby fast-food places, finishing with the reminder, "Afternoon workshops start promptly at one-thirty. Don't be late."

Outside, the glare from the white stucco buildings sent Val hunting for her sunglasses. She took a deep breath of salt-scented air, wishing she were going to the university in the fall instead of Miramar. She loved the location.

Santa Theresa University perched on a point overlooking the Pacific, with the Santa Ynez mountains to the north. Spread out like the spokes of a wheel, the buildings were primarily Spanish style with red-tiled roofs, arched openings, and colorful mosaics.

But Nell was oblivious to anything but Dirk. "Would you believe that guy! Typical Miramar preppie!" She squinted at the bronze sculpture of a diver in front of the Arts Building. "This doesn't look familiar. Where are we?"

"How can anything look familiar when you can't see?" Val guided her to a blue-tiled walkway leading to their dorm.

"Don't change the subject." Nell finally found her prescription sunglasses. "Tell me you're not going to be taken in by him. Especially that phony smile."

"Give him a break." Val opened the door of their dorm. "You don't even know him."

"I know his type."

Once Nell made up her mind it took an act of God to change it, so Val didn't even try. Upstairs they found the rest of their dorm group sprawled in the hall eating pizza.

Hal Corrigan, a senior from San Jose, greeted them.

"Too hot in those closets they call rooms." He held up two pepperoni-and-mushroom slices. "Want some?"

"And how."

Both Val and Nell founds spots on the floor, and after contributing to the food fund, they began comparing notes with the others on the morning's seminars. Since most of the kids came from different California schools, they were still getting acquainted. Although the girls were lodged on one side of the dorm and the boys on the other, they spent most of their waking hours together.

"Sorry to hear about your school closing. That must have been rough," a chubby blonde with braces sympathized.

"Tell me about it." Nell was still bitter.

"The worst is not being able to graduate from Winona," Val admitted. "I mean, when you get to be a senior, you think you have it made, and then suddenly you've got to start all over again on a new campus."

"Like being a freshman again," Nell complained.

The blonde shuddered. "Nothing could be that bad."

Everyone laughed, but Val could feel their concern and it helped.

Hal crumpled one of the empty pizza boxes and tossed it into the waste bin. "Have you guys been over to your new campus yet?"

"It's ugly." Nell was still fighting the move.

"It's older." Val tried to be fair, but she had to admit she'd miss Winona's green lawns and rose garden. Miramar buildings were closely clustered, with more concrete and fewer trees.

"You'll get to like Miramar if you give it a chance."

Vall turned and recognized Karen Wexler, the senior who was Miramar's choice for treasurer. Beneath shaggy brown hair, she had gray-green eyes with the longest eyelashes Val had ever seen.

"We know we could have been closed instead of you, so we do understand. And we want you to feel welcome."

She seemed sincere but Nell wasn't buying it. "That's not what I heard! Word is that we're referred to as the immigrant invasion."

Karen looked uncomfortable. "Some of the kids do feel the school will be overcrowded now," she admitted. "And, well, Winona's always had the reputation for being . . . rowdy."

"So that's why Dirk came on so strong!" Nell pretended to finally understand. "He's anticipating a campus riot come September."

"No, you've got him all wrong! He's a great guy and he's done a lot for the school." Karen's defense was so strong, Val wondered if they had something going.

As if she read Val's mind, Karen asked, "What's your impression of Dirk?"

Val brushed the crumbs off her shorts. "He seems rather sure of himself."

"So was Napoleon," Nell remarked.

"That's not fair," Karen objected. "You don't even know him."

"Don't want to either." Nell half rose to leave, but Val pulled her back down.

"Hey, take it easy." She handed each of them some more pizza. Food always had a soothing effect on Nell, but Karen still looked upset.

Val appealed to her. "Look, I want to get along with Dirk, but he has to understand it's an equal partnership. Both of us were elected in our own right. Now that the two schools are one, we're joint leaders."

"He knows that and he really does want the campus to be unified." Karen assured her.

Val hoped so. To her relief the subject was dropped, and soon it was time for the afternoon workshops. Nell had already gone ahead with Hal when Karen fell into step beside Val.

"Maybe I shouldn't push it," Karen began, "but you seem, well, more open-minded than your friend."

"Oh, Nell's all right," Val defended her. "She's still angry about the closure, that's all. It makes her touchy."

"I guess I'd feel the same way. But I really admire your attitude. You're looking forward, not back."

Val stopped staring at the blue mosaics underfoot and looked at Karen. They both smiled, and Val wondered if maybe the Miramar kids wouldn't be so bad after all.

They turned right at the Humanities Wing, stopping to admire the mural of Don Quixote.

Then Karen asked abruptly, "Can I give you some advice?"

"Sure." Val was always ready to listen, though she usually made up her own mind.

"Give Dirk a chance. Maybe he is used to running the show his way, but he's been in student government since sophomore year and, believe me, he's had to work with some losers." She stopped to remove a pebble from her sandal. "Anyway, what I'm trying to say is he's a great guy. He's just learned that if you want something done, you do it yourself."

That was nothing new to Val. Last year she was only supposed to assist the commissioner of entertainment, and ended up running Spring Week single-handedly.

"When he sees how competent you are, he'll be glad to share the work," Karen assured her.

Val didn't like the idea of having to prove herself. The fact that she was elected should be proof enough. She slowed her steps. Who was she kidding? Most of the students voted more on popularity than ability.

She smiled at Karen, who was still looking worried.

"I'm sure Dirk and I'll get along just fine."

Crossing her fingers, she went into the workshop. Their counselor was a string bean of a guy with long arms and a bobbing Adam's apple.

He paced across the front of the classroom. "What I'd like to do this afternoon is see how you handle some typical situations."

Val felt a prickle of nervousness, which increased when she was the first to be chosen. She rubbed her sweaty hands on her shorts.

He smiled, trying to put her at ease. "Suppose, as student body president, you have someone working with you who's undependable. Never shows up on time . . ." he waved his hand as if pulling ideas from the air. "Promises a lot but never delivers . . ."

"Sounds familiar," Hal muttered.

The leader agreed. "Unfortunately, yes." He turned back to Val. "How would you handle this?"

She thought for a minute. "First, I'd try talking to him alone. You know, make him realize he's letting everyone down."

"But if he's irresponsible, would that work?" the leader asked.

"Probably not," Val had to admit. "So maybe I'd put him in charge of something, like a school tournament or publicity. Then if he blew it, he'd have to take the heat."

"Drastic," the leader acknowledged, "but certainly well deserved." He looked around the room. "Any other ideas?"

Nell didn't hesitate. "Impeach him!"

"Ignore him," suggested the blonde with the braces.

"But we want him to learn something," the leader objected. "Grow from the experience. Kicking him out would only make him angry, and then he'd probably end up blaming others rather than seeing it's his own fault."

"That's why I think he should be responsible for something." Val liked the poetic justice of her idea. "Who can he blame but himself if it's a disaster?"

"He'd find someone," Dirk remarked. "Why not bring up the problem at a group meeting?" His words came fast, as if they had trouble keeping pace with his thoughts. "Don't single him out or anything, but maybe admit you've always had a problem getting things done. Then who knows? He might have the guts to say he does too."

"Good thinking," the leader said. "I like the nonblaming factor." Hands in his pockets, he hunched his thin shoulders as if to squeeze out his thoughts. "Also, if you can get the others in the group to admit how they feel when he lets them down rather than blame him, you could go a long way toward making him a productive member rather than alienating him."

Val had to admit Dirk's solution was sound, and she wished she'd thought of it herself.

Dirk slanted her a humorous look. "Not that I buy the idea of the do-nothing being a he. Let's have some equal rights here."

Sharp whistles mingled with boos greeted his comment, and Val acknowledged his dig with a nod. He'd won the first round, but years of sparring with her brothers had taught her resilience. Wait till next time.

But they didn't meet again until that evening, when he sat down beside her on the lawn. It was unwinding time, but the counselors had not yet started the cheers. Wearing a green sweater against the ocean breeze, Dirk looked disturbingly handsome.

"Thought we should get to know each other."
The stern line of his lips softened in a smile.
"After all, we'll be working together all year."

"Good idea." Val was glad she was sitting down.
At close range, he had a powerful effect on her.

He stretched out his long legs. "I liked the
way you handled yourself today."

She bristled. "High praise coming from you."
Who did he think he was, the counselor or
something?

Dirk hit his head with the heel of his hand. "I
did it again, didn't I?"

Her anger evaporated at his comic dismay.
"Terminal foot-in-mouth disease, my brothers
call it."

"How many brothers do you have?" He looked
interested.

"Three," she sighed. "All older."

Dirk grinned. "You must have been a tough
kid to survive that."

"My Dad says we're evenly matched."

He raised his head. "Is that a warning?"

"Depends on whether you intend to lead or
follow." She might as well get it out into the
open.

"How about a little of both?"

"As long as it works both ways, partner." She
held out her hand but found herself succumbing
to his smile and his touch.

"Val Robinson." His hand moved in hers, de-
molishing all her defenses. "This promises to be
one challenging year."

She didn't deny it, and when she joined in the
group cheer, Val found she was looking forward
to September with far more enthusiasm than
she'd ever dreamed possible.

Chapter Two

Val continued to run into Dirk at seminars, but too many people and too little time prevented more than casual conversation. She spent most of her days with the dorm group anyway, and aside from waving to him while crossing campus or exchanging a few words on the breakfast hike, the week passed without her getting to know him better.

On the last day, good-byes were said, letters promised, and then she was heading for the parking lot where the familiar green Mustang sportscar waited. Naturally, Joe was behind the wheel. At twenty, he could always be counted on to chauffeur without complaint, finish abandoned chores, and man the barbecue in her father's absence.

Easygoing, with a ready smile, he was slow to anger but the family soon learned not to push him too far. When he had become fed up with Jim's unlicensed borrowing, Joe had quietly retaliated by wiping out his brother's horde of macadamia nuts. Jim kept clear of him after that.

When Joe saw Val coming, he got out of the car and she noticed he'd had his hair cut. It lay close to his head like a brown cap.

"So how'd it go?" He tossed her bag into the trunk.

Val eased herself onto the hot vinyl seat, careful not to burn her bare legs. "Great. I met all sorts of new people." She wondered why he didn't get into the car. "So let's go."

"Isn't Nell coming?"

She'd forgotten he had a crush on her. "Are you kidding? Half the male population's in there right now fighting to drive her home."

Joe got behind the wheel. "And no one asked you?" He grinned. "What's the problem? Bad breath?"

"No, warts!" she retorted. "You know, you guys do wonders for my ego."

"Keeps you honest." The car stalled as usual, and he patiently restarted it.

"When are you going to trade in this antique for a car that runs?"

"If it's so bad, why do you borrow it all the time?" He had her there. Joe was pretty generous letting her use it to drive to school when he was at college, especially since he treated it more like a pet than a vehicle of transportation.

A car honked and Dirk waved to her before he cut across them and sped out of the parking lot. Karen was sitting next to him.

"Who's the speed freak?" Joe muttered. Dirk's maneuver had forced him to brake sharply, killing the engine.

"He's my co-president from Miramar." She watched his car disappear around the corner.

"You two get along?" The engine finally caught and Joe drove into the street.

"We had a few skirmishes," she admitted, remembering some of Dirk's high-handed remarks.

"You win?"

"I'd call it a draw."

Joe looked impressed. "He must be tough." He avoided the busy shopping streets and swung into the thickly shaded residential area. "But my money's on you."

It was nice to hear, but she had no illusions about Dirk. No matter how readily he'd agreed to their partnership that night on the lawn, he had a mind of his own. But then so did she, and Val wasn't about to follow tamely where Dirk Atwood chose to lead.

Still, she couldn't deny he was attractive. As Joe turned into Calle del Loro, Val wondered if Dirk and Karen were going together. Giving her a lift home didn't mean much.

In spite of what she'd told Joe, Val could have gotten a ride with Ray Lazell. Winona's student body vice-president, Ray was a tall, lanky, sandy-haired guy whose passion was music, and particularly his brother's band. They'd been dating on and off since last year, but more for convenience than anything else. He had a gentleness Val found appealing, combined with loyalty and persistence.

"Here we are." Joe parked in the driveway of their two-storied Spanish-style house, which boasted a round tower, pitched tile roof, and wrought iron balconies. Val loved the white stucco walls and wide arches connecting the rooms. No place was cooler in summer, and the stone fireplaces made it cosy in winter.

Kicking off her shoes in the hall to feel the unglazed tiles beneath her feet, Val ran through the living room into the kitchen searching for her mother. She wanted to tell her about the camp. But it turned out that her father was back and was describing his flight to Hawaii to Val's mom.

"Would you believe some clod hit the chute button on the exit door and it took them an hour to refold it? Then he had the gall to complain we were late." An airline pilot, he came and went at odd hours. Fortunately, Val's mother disliked routine and managed to put together meals at a moment's notice.

"Have some wine and relax," she suggested. A small woman, she asserted herself when necessary, and her blue eyes could be annoyingly perceptive when Val had something to hide. Her children both adored and towered over her, particularly Ralph, now well over six feet.

At twenty-two he could shoot a basket or outswim the best athlete, but was more interested in politics than sports. When he saw Val, he let out a whoop and lifted her off her feet. The most physical of her brothers, Ralph was also the worst tease.

"Don't bruise the merchandise," she ordered, clinging helplessly as he spun her around.

He set her on her feet. "Packaging shows a few bulges," he observed. Ralph was the Robinson connoisseur of the female figure.

"Who wants to date a bag of bones?" Val carried the chicken and rice to the table.

"Who wants to date a ten-ton truck?" Ralph retorted, racing Jim for the chair nearest the chicken.

Her mother lifted her glass and tapped it with a spoon. "End of round one. Now settle down and eat."

Food shut the boys up long enough for Val to

tell her parents about leadership camp. Dirk seemed to provoke the most comment.

"Sounds like he wants to be in charge." Ralph reached for another biscuit. "Think he might try to ace you out?"

"Not when he discovers her left hook." Jim grinned and ducked when Val half rose from her seat.

Her father advised, "Don't let Dirk push you around."

"I'd like to see him try," Jim muttered.

"Beat him at his own game." Ralph took more rice. "Show him what a Winona Tiger can do."

"Yeah. Run those Miramar Wildcats into the ground," Jim urged. Formerly on the Winona football team, he'd played some rough games with the Miramar Wildcats. All the Robinson kids had graduated from Winona. All except Val.

"That's a nice, open-minded attitude," her mother remarked. "I'm sure Val would be willing to compromise at times."

"Just not all the time." Val would not let Dirk's compelling ways and slow grin overpower her.

Removing the last chicken leg from Ralph's reach, Val's mother passed it to her husband. "Why not wait and see what happens when school starts."

Unfortunately, school started long before Val was ready. What with her waitress job at the Feed Bag and seeing Nell, the summer slipped by. Ray still called, but she dated him less frequently, preferring to hang around with the crowd. Lately Val found she had less patience with the woes of his brother's band; she preferred not being alone with him.

All too soon it was September—the end of her summer job and the beginning of school. Since Val had never found time to familiarize herself with the Miramar campus, the first day of school left her lost and too embarrassed to ask for help.

"I'm homesick already," she confessed to Nell, trying to locate her government class on the school map.

"Talk about the Twilight Zone." Nell eyed the knots of students around her. "Get a load of those designer clothes."

"You think we look all right?" Val smoothed her wraparound skirt and matching pink blouse.

"We'd outclass them any day." But Val noticed that even Nell had needed the security of her contact lenses today.

She sighed as she looked around. Would she ever feel at home? The campus seemed a concrete maze with steps and walks going in all directions. She finally located her class in a two-storied building overlooking the parking lot.

"See you later," she called to Nell.

"I hope."

The rest of the day wasn't much better. Val was usually late for class, and even though the teachers sympathized, they were unfamiliar and unknown to her. When she found she had a math class with a former Winona teacher, she felt as if she'd come home.

By the end of the day, Val was exhausted and in no mood to co-chair her first student council meeting, especially when she and Nell couldn't find the room.

But Karen came to their rescue. "Come with me. I'll show you the way," she offered. Her green dress had a Pierre Cardin logo and a style

that did great things for her figure. "Didn't want
you ending up in the boys' locker room." She
led them down one of the walkways behind the
library.

"Don't bring up the past," Val had been gull-
ible enough to fall into the trap and still cringed
at the memory.

Karen stopped. "You're kidding! You too?"

They started to laugh but Nell didn't seem
amused. "We'd better get a move on or we'll be
late."

Val looked at her in surprise. Usually Nell loved
a good joke, but she hadn't said much since
Karen appeared. Maybe she'd had a rough day.

Val gave her a poke. "Wish me luck."

Nell's dimples appeared. "You got it, prez."

Karen opened a door to a carpeted room with
long tables forming a T. Dirk was already seated
and waved Val over.

"Have you met our student activities director,
Mr. Weymouth?" He indicated a burly man
whose close-cropped hair accentuated his bullet-
shaped head.

"Good to have you on the team." Mr. Weymouth's handshake was strong. "We all pull together here and want you people from Winona
to feel at home. So whenever you guys want to
call a play, feel free to get it off your chest."

Val wanted to ask how many years he'd been
coaching football, but merely thanked him and
took her place beside Dirk. Karen had warned
her that Miramar used Robert's Rules of Order
to run meetings, but Val figured they'd be used
as casually as at Winona. She was wrong.

Amost immediately after Dirk opened the
meeting, a tall redheaded guy took the floor.

"Madam President. Mr. President."

Dirk handed her the gavel to recognize him, but Val couldn't remember his name. She'd met so many new people. Everyone waited and she felt the perspiration on her back and hands.

Dirk retrieved the gavel. "Chair recognizes Tim Merrick."

Val knew she'd have to be on her toes from now on. To the Miramar kids she was an unknown, and would only get their support if she proved herself. At least she knew Ray and Nell were in her corner. Reassured, she returned her attention to Tim.

"I make a motion we discuss the first pep rally to kick off the football season."

His pun drew groans from Nell and Merrie, but the Miramars seemed either bored or used to Tim's humor. Robyn, the slim blonde who shared the vice-presidency with Ray, seconded the motion, but as Dirk reached for the gavel, Val beat him to it.

"I move we accept the resolution to discuss the first pep rally."

She suspected Dirk didn't like her taking over and was positive when the silence lengthened and he made no effort to help. Everyone was waiting for her to do something. But what?

It was Dirk who finally supplied the answer. "Is the motion seconded?"

Val owed him one for that. He'd enjoyed watching her squirm. But if he thought she would sit back tamely and let him run the whole show, he was sadly mistaken. What she needed to do now was get those rules of order down cold so he wouldn't have an advantage.

Karen had been recognized by the chair, and

she opened the debate. "We don't have much time to get ready for the first game Friday, so what about holding the rally during lunch that day?" Her long nails skimmed the edge of the table. "It will get the kids up for the game and we want a big turnout."

Nell interrupted. "No one comes during lunch. At Winona, we always had a special rally schedule."

"You're out of order, Nell," Dirk ruled. "Karen has the floor."

Val held her breath, praying she would not tell him what he could do with his rules. But for once, Nell didn't speak again till she took the floor officially.

With her face flushed and her blonde hair tumbling about her shoulders, she had everyone's attention. "We want the whole school at this rally, right?" Val and Ray nodded. "So let's hold it when everyone will come. Not at lunch."

Tim took the floor again. "We've always had rallies during lunch at Miramar. Here the teachers don't like having their classes interrupted by rally schedules."

His know-it-all attitude caused Val to forget the rules. She broke in. "We're not asking for a rally schedule every day. Just when there's a game." Dirk raised his gavel, but Val ignored him. "At Winona, we tried rallies during lunch, and everyone just took off." She appealed to them. "I mean, let's face it. We may have a closed campus, but when we have extended lunch everyone's off to McDonald's."

Even some of the Miramar kids laughed, and for the first time, Val felt she was making progress.

Then Dirk stepped in. "You're out of order, Val. Tim has the floor."

She could feel her face getting hot and didn't know where to look. Even when the president made a mistake at Winona, no one called him on it, except maybe in a kidding way. But Dirk wasn't kidding, and the fact that he was right made it worse.

When Tim was through, Nell quickly got the floor. "Val's right," she said loyally. "If we really want to get some school spirit around here, we need the kids at the rally. And the only way to get them is to shorten third and fourth periods so we can have the rally in between." She shrugged. "It'll only mean about ten minutes off each class."

"You can't get the whole school to a rally and back in twenty-five minutes," Tim argued when he was recognized.

"So you cut a few more minutes off." Nell hated being pinned down by details. "The point is the rally should be held between classes, not at lunch!"

Mr. Weymouth was appealed to and he pronounced the words Val was already coming to hate. "We've always done it this way at Miramar, always had rallies at lunch."

"So what? Maybe it's time for a change." Val didn't care if she was out of order.

"Why? You're saying there's something wrong with Miramar?" Dirk sounded defensive.

"Not exactly. But there's always room for change."

Apparently the Miramar students did not think so, for when Dirk called for a vote, they all supported rallies at lunch. Naturally the Winonas opposed the idea, and the council was split.

Dirk looked at Val and she knew if they voted together, they could break the tie. "We don't want to split the campus," he urged.

Val doubted if that would happen but tested how far he would go. "You can prevent it if you vote for a rally schedule," she pointed out.

His surprise proved he thought she'd fold. He obviously didn't know her very well. Having made no decision, the council agreed to discuss the rally again the next day and adjourned the meeting.

When Val saw Dirk go over to some of the Winona kids, she wondered if he would try to sway their votes. Nell was sure of it and fumed all the way to the parking lot.

"Can you believe that guy? Not only is he dropping rules all over the place, now he's trying to infiltrate our group."

Val had to agree. "I don't see what's so terrible about a rally schedule anyway." After unlocking Joe's car, she sat for a moment trying to compose herself. The last thing she wanted was an accident.

"It's not the way we do things at Miramar," Nell mimicked as she slammed the door.

"Watch it," Val warned. "This is Joe's baby, remember?"

"Sorry, But you know as well as I do what's going to happen. He'll get to some of those geeks who'll believe anything and convince them to change their votes."

"Like Merrie Tillman?" Val thought of the shy student body secretary and knew she'd collapse like a house of cards. Merrie hardly ever dated and Dirk could be awfully persuasive when he put his mind to it.

"Yeah. Or Josh Dykzeuil." Nell had hated him since second grade when he'd put green ink in her hair. She'd dubbed him the "Wimp of Winona," and neither of them could understand how he'd made co-treasurer with Karen. "What we need is some new ammunition," Nell decided.

"Sure, but what? Mr. Weymouth's no help. He's one hundred percent pro-Miramar." After stalling Joe's car twice, Val finally managed to drive out of the parking lot and make a left turn onto Almendro Drive.

"I got it!" Nell shouted. "Who's got more clout than the student council or Mr. Weymouth?" She didn't give Val time to answer. "The principal, right?"

"Mr. Harris?" Val braked sharply, and the engine promptly died. She honked at the two teenaged drivers ahead whose Volkswagen cars were blocking the road as they talked. "Why get him involved?"

"Don't you see? Their big argument is that teachers won't go for the rally schedule." Nell twisted in her seat so she could face Val, who was maneuvering around the unmoving cars. "But if the principal okays it, what can they do?"

It all sounded so simple the way Nell put it. But then, her ideas usually did. The problems usually surfaced when someone was trying to put them into action.

"And who's to propose this to the principal?" Val inquired.

"Who else but Madam Prez?"

"Thanks." Val turned right onto Calle del Pajaro

and parked near a clump of silver dollar gum trees, the circular leaves silver in the sun. "I've got to give it some thought. Going over people's heads is risky. Sure you may win one battle, but you can also lose the war."

"If we lose the first battle, there'll be no more war to fight," Nell argued.

But Val wouldn't be pushed. "Let me sleep on it, okay?"

"Okay." Nell gathered up her books and got out of the car. "Remember, the Winonas are depending on you." She closed the door. "Thanks for the lift."

"See you later." Thoughtfully, Val drove the few remaining blocks to her home. She still didn't like the idea of going over Dirk's head. And she knew he wouldn't like it either. But what other choice did she have? He would have the votes tomorrow unless she could come up with something. Nell was right. With the principal behind them, she was sure they'd get the rally schedule passed.

Val walked slowly up to the house. If only she didn't have to go over Dirk's head. Maybe if she called him, tried to explain—but Nell would call that alerting the enemy. What should she do? She didn't want him as an enemy. Maybe that was why she resisted going to the principal.

She sighed. No matter how attracted she was to Dirk, Val mustn't let her feelings interfere with what she thought was right. The question was, What was right?

Chapter Three

But her brothers had no problem making a decision.

"You go to the principal." Ralph closed the refrigerator door with a decisive snap and set the ham, mustard, and cheese on the counter. They were all in the kitchen fixing a late-night snack. "Remember the time I got into a hassle over running the senior prom?" he asked.

"Yeah." Val broke off a piece of cheese. "The vice-principal—"

"Dickson the dictator," Joe broke in.

"—cut off your funds."

Ralph pointed his knife at Val. "Did I sit back and take it?"

She had to admit he hadn't.

"No. I went down to the PTA and got the money from them. You should have seen Dickson's face when I told him I didn't need his money." A satisfied smile spread over Ralph's face. "One of my many truly great moves."

"But this is different," Val insisted, trying to turn his mind from his own brilliance to her problem. "You had all the kids behind you. I don't. The Miramars voted against the rally schedule too, remember?"

"The Miramars or Dirk?" Joe removed his

toasted cheese sandwich from the microwave and sat down beside her at the counter.

Val avoided his eyes. "Don't be dumb. What do I care how Dirk voted?" She hoped she sounded convincing.

"If it's not the guy," Jim observed from his place in front of the portable TV, "it must be you. Scared to go see the principal?" he challenged

"I've heard about him," Ralph added.

Joe looked at her. "Rules with an iron hand."

"That is not the reason!" Val glared at them.

Finishing his sandwich, Ralph leaned over the counter. "Okay, here's how I see it. Either you go to the principal and fix Dirk's clock, or you give in and become his shadow the rest of the year. His yes-man. Sure will make the Winonas glad they elected you."

"Don't bully Val," her mother ordered, removing the ham and cheese before Ralph could make a second sandwich. "She has to do what she thinks is right." Her mother cautioned Val. "If you have any doubts about going to the principal, don't."

She did have doubts. Lots of them. How would Dirk react if she went over his head? After all, she did have to work with him for a year. No sense alienating him right off. Besides, she had no guarantee the principal would even go for a rally schedule.

But did she have any choice? If she was going to accomplish anything at Miramar, she had to assert herself right away. The kids made up their minds pretty fast and Val wanted their respect. But how would they react if she went to the principal?

Val went up to bed still undecided and dreamed she was being pursued by an unknown enemy. She felt him behind her, coming closer. Running down a long corridor, she found two doors. Somehow she knew something awful was behind one. She froze. The footsteps came closer. She had to do something!

Val woke up sweating and had to go downstairs for some milk before she could sleep again. As a result, she didn't hear the alarm and barely made it to her first period class. Not that she learned much. She spent the entire time mentally debating the pros and cons of seeing the principal, instead of watching the filmstrip on the Supreme Court.

She needed to talk to someone, but had missed Nell because she'd been late and now couldn't find her during snack. Usually, Nell was first in line for food during the fifteen-minute morning break, but not today. Her eyes on the food lines, Val wasn't watching where she was going and slammed into Dirk.

"You must be hungry." He grinned, his hands on her shoulders to steady her.

For a moment, Val forgot the vote, the principal, and the rally. All she could think of was that she never wanted him to let go.

Naturally, he did. Val searched desperately for something clever to say, so he wouldn't suspect his effect on her. She couldn't think of a thing.

Meanwhile he'd bought two milks and some cinnamon rolls, sharing them with her. "I looked for you before school."

Val couldn't believe it. He was interested! Didn't he buy her breakfast? "I overslept." Why hadn't she worn her new skirt instead of her old sweats? "Was it anything special?" They ducked under the rail and found a place on the grass.

His hair looked chestnut in the morning sun and the wind kept tossing it into his eyes. Impatiently, he pushed it back. "I wanted to talk to you about the pep rally."

The bun lost its flavor. It was business after all. How could she be so dumb! After all, he barely knew her.

"We need to get it off the ground," he urged. Her continued silence seemed to be making him curious.

"Right," she said quickly, not wanting him to guess her thoughts.

Finishing his cinnamon bun, he leaned back, propping his body on his elbows. "I know the situation's rough for you guys. I mean, coming to a new school and all. Give me that." He took her empty milk container and tossed it into the bin. "But I think," he settled down next to her again, "once we all start working together, it'll be better."

"Sure it will." She knew what he was trying to say. He was going to change his vote.

Dirk sat up. "So, what do you say we patch up our differences today at the council and present a united front?"

Val never dreamed he'd give in so easily. "Sounds good to me."

"Terrific." The confident grin was back. "I knew you'd come around. Karen wasn't so sure, but I told her that once you had a chance to think it over, you'd make the right decision."

Val had the same feeling she'd encountered when her history teacher quizzed her on the one chapter she hadn't read. But when she opened her mouth to speak, he stopped her.

"No, you don't have to explain. I understand. You wanted to make an impression at the meeting yesterday. Frankly," he grinned, "I would have done the same in your place. I admired you for it. But now with your vote for lunch rallies, we'll have a majority."

Val choked on her bun. What did he mean, with her vote for lunch rallies? She'd never said that. But again he didn't give her a chance to speak.

"And don't worry about the other Winonas on the council." He was on his feet now. "Once they see how successful our rallies can be, they'll come around. It's only a matter of time." He ducked under the rail. "See you later." His head at a cocky angle, Dirk headed down the crowded walkway before she could set him straight.

Val stared after him, too furious to move. So that's why he was looking for her. Not to get to know her better, but to brainwash her. How could he? Val wished she hadn't eaten his food. She felt like she'd swallowed a bribe.

The bell rang but she didn't care if she was late for class. In fact, she wasn't going to class. She was going to see the principal!

Before she could change her mind, she ducked under the rail and hurried toward the administration building. Students jammed the walks trying to get to class, and Val longed for the less crowded Winona campus.

She climbed three steps and entered the cream-colored building whose corridor led past the attendance and counseling offices. She'd only been here once, when she'd registered. The principal's office was at the end. His secretary was away from her desk but, peeking through the door, Val spotted Mr. Harris. He looked up.

"You looking for me?" He was a heavy-set man nearing retirement age, with a decisive air and commanding voice. He was far different from her old principal, who had a friendly word for everyone.

Anger made her bold. "I wanted to talk about Friday's pep rally." She walked into his office but remained standing. "For a good turnout, we really need a special schedule."

He remained silent, giving no indication of whether he approved or not

Val's voice became more anxious. "You see, if the rally could be mandatory and held between third and fourth periods, everyone would have to come."

"The gym wouldn't hold everyone."

She wouldn't let him dismiss the idea so quickly. "So we have it on the football field," she suggested. "The kids could sit in the stands. You know, we really could use some school spirit around here."

He frowned and Val realized he probably thought she was knocking his school.

"Not that Miramar hasn't spirit already," she added hastily. "I just meant—"

"I know what you meant." He pointed to a chair and she sat. "What we're facing this year is the problem of joining two rival schools. It'll be difficult, but I intend to see that nothing interferes with that unity." He spoke slowly and each word carried authority. "What I won't stand for is a divided school."

He seemed to be warning her and Val hurried

to reassure him. "That's why I want a rally schedule. So we can get everyone there."

He thought it over for a few minutes. Val inspected the framed pictures of former student body presidents on the walls. Most of them were boys.

"All right, we'll give it a try. Friday we'll have a special schedule."

She could hardly believe it. He'd agreed! All she had to do now was convince the council. And that shouldn't be hard with the principal's backing. But first she wanted to find Dirk. Val had a score to settle with him and eventually tracked him down on the way to the meeting. She gave him the good news.

"YOU DID WHAT!" His face was becoming an alarming shade of red.

"Went to the principal and he okayed the schedule." She pretended surprise. "Why? Wasn't that your main objection? That the teachers wouldn't like it?" Val beamed. "Now, with the principal behind the schedule . . ." She left him to fill in the rest.

"But you said you were going to vote for lunch rallies," he accused her.

"No, that's what you said," she pointed out. "I didn't have a chance to say anything." His high-handedness still rankled.

"Well, you certainly found enough to say to the principal." His sarcasm was evident. "Or is that how you usually operate? Behind someone's back."

"I would have told you but you took off." That wasn't entirely true, but he was making her defensive.

"How convenient. Did you always run to the

principal when you didn't get your way at Winona?"

That hurt. "No, and you don't think so either."

"I don't know what to think." He turned away toward the council room but Val ran after him.

"Look, we both want the same thing," she urged. "A successful rally. And I really believe this is the only way."

The stubborn lines around his jaw deepened. "What you're really saying is that no matter what it takes, you're going to get what you want."

"That's not fair," she objected.

"You're a fine one to talk about fair." His voice was rising. "Who went over our heads? Who got the principal's okay without even bothering to discuss it with me or the student council?"

She felt like a hostile witness being cross-examined by the prosecuting attorney, and she didn't like it. "That's what really bugs you, isn't it?" she retorted. "That you weren't consulted. Maybe if you had a more open mind I would have talked to you first." Val turned her back on him but felt his hands on her shoulders yanking her around.

"Now you listen to me!" he ordered.

"No! You listen!" Val tried to get free but he was too strong, which only infuriated her more. "You just assumed I'd go along with whatever you wanted. Buy the sucker some food, turn on the charm, and she'll jump through any hoop you want." He tried to interrupt but she was too wound up. "Let me tell you, President Atwood, I have a mind of my own and I intend to use it!"

"No one has to tell me that." He sounded bitter. "Too bad you can't put that mind of yours on what's good for the school and not yourself."

With that parting shot, he released her and walked off in the direction of the student council room. Val had no desire to follow but had no choice. The meeting would be sticky and she needed to defend her actions if she wanted the rally schedule approved. Suddenly she was almost at the meeting room and slowed her steps.

What really hurt was that Dirk saw her as selfish when all she wanted was to make Miramar a place where the Winonas could feel at home. What was wrong with that? If Miramar wanted any kind of school spirit, they had to accept some Winona ideas. Otherwise, the Winonas would never feel a part of their new school.

Nothing selfish about that, she told herself, and went into the meeting with her head held high. Dirk fought her every inch of the way, but the principal's approval swayed enough Miramar votes to get the rally schedule accepted.

He didn't look happy. "Okay, then, it's up to the commissioners of entertainment to get it off the ground." He directed his words at Nell and Tim. "Naturally, the rest of us will help wherever needed." Then he adjourned the meeting and left without a word to Val.

She told herself she didn't care. Right now she faced a more immediate problem: Nell and Tim. They sat glaring at each other across the council table. Unless she could get them to work together, the rally was doomed from the start.

"Okay, you guys," she announced. "Let's split the work three ways." At least then she could act as referee. "What do we need first?"

"You think you can handle the band?" Nell

asked Tim skeptically. "I mean, we need them to open it."

"I think I can manage that." His freckles stood out prominently when he was annoyed. Now they reminded Val of flashing red lights. She intervened swiftly.

"Great. I'll talk to the drill team and pep club."

"You'll need tapes of their music too," Nell reminded her.

"Right." Val made a note. "Will you handle the relays?" She knew if anyone could get volunteers, it would be Nell.

"Sure, and I'll work with Robyn on the signs."

"Why?" Tim was still smarting from Nell's earlier skepticism. "Don't you think she can handle her job either?" He was becoming defensive of the Miramar officers.

Nell didn't help. "I don't know. Can she?"

Val cut in quickly. "Of course she can."

But Tim wasn't ready to drop it. "This isn't the first rally we've ever done, you know."

"But now that we're here, it'll be the best," countered Nell. "Ready, Val?"

"Thanks for your help, Tim." Val smiled. "Let me know if there's anything more I can do."

He buried his head in his backpack and didn't answer.

"Great help he's going to be," grumbled Nell when they were outside.

"Try to get along, will you?" Val was making mental lists of what still had to be done. They didn't have much time.

"Sure, sure." They stopped for a moment to watch the pep club work out, before turning toward the parking lot. "Who's going to talk to the janitors about the sound system?" Nell made a face. "I don't even know where the maintenance department is."

"I'll find it." Val had another thought. "Get Merrie to help with those signs. She's pretty artistic."

"Stop being a worrywart," Nell urged. "You'll see. It'll be a smash."

"I hope so." Val told herself all she cared about was the school spirit, but knew she wanted to prove to Dirk that she'd been right. And do that, the rally had to be a success.

By Friday she was irritable, tense, and jumpy. Nor did facing twenty-four hundred students help. When she saw them filing into the stands she wanted to run, but stood her ground as she saw Dirk watching. She was surprised he even came.

The band finished playing and Val walked up to the mike. She prayed her voice wouldn't crack.

"Good to have all of you here for our first big rally of the year. The game's tonight and we want to show everyone that the Miramar Wildcats are the best football team ever!"

The pep club gave a cheer but Val didn't hear much enthusiasm from the stands. Some kids were throwing paper airplanes and other's were still looking for seats. No one seemed particularly involved. Val hurried to introduce the drill team.

"Let's have a big hand for our girls in blue," she encouraged as the team marched on the field, each girl carrying a small bamboo baton with a white ribbon attached to it. Nell turned on their tape and they went into a succession of leaps, spins, and backward dance steps to make the ribbons swirl about them.

Val worried they'd run over their allotted time, and kept looking at her watch. Whatever happened, they had to stick to the schedule. The principal had made that very clear to her. With relief, she saw them finish and was so eager to carry on that she hardly noticed the slight applause.

"Okay, listen up, you guys!" she announced. "We're going to start the relays now to see which team can pop the balloon and open the gum inside."

She turned to instruct the teams and was amazed to see Dirk pitted against Nell. Whatever happened between them, he was obviously going to show a united front. She appreciated that.

"Okay, as soon as one of you gets the gum open and in your mouth, run to the end of the line. Then the next person goes. First team through wins. Ready? Let's go!"

Wearing gloves did not make balloon breaking or gum unwrapping any easier, but Dirk managed to get ahead of Nell.

"Go, Nell, go!"

"ALL RIGHT, DIRK!"

Val kept hoping the kids in the stands would get into the spirit, but most of the cheers came from the student council and pep club.

When the relay ended, she had just enough time to do the competitive cheers.

"Let's hear it, freshmen!" she yelled and taught them the cheer. "Shout M for Mira and clap three times, M again for Mar and clap, then H, then S. MMHS FIGHT FIGHT FIGHT!"

As usual the freshmen were disorganized, giggly, and less forceful than the rowdy sophomores. But even the stonger efforts of the juniors and seniors were nothing like the ear-splitting rallies she'd known at Winona.

When it was over, Val felt relieved but depressed. She didn't know what she'd done wrong, but knew it hadn't come off. Usually kids came by after a rally to congratulate her, but today no one came. No one but Dirk.

He walked across the field to where she stood. Val wondered if he'd come to gloat.

Chapter Four

As Val waited, instinctively on the defensive, Dirk's eyes crinkled.

"You expecting a fight?"

"Maybe." She was wary.

He began gathering the paper airplanes thrown on the field. "I thought I'd give you a hand."

"The maintenance men will take care of that." She hadn't meant to sound ungrateful but he immediately straightened.

"Yeah, sure."

Val thought he'd go then, but he just stood looking across the field. He was making her nervous.

"I'd better get to class," she muttered, but he stopped her.

"You did a good job."

Something broke inside and she turned on him. "So why was it a bomb?"

He looked exasperated. "Because it's too soon, because the kids don't know each other, because half of them don't want to be here, because—"

"Okay, okay." She held up her hands. "You don't have to shout."

His mouth had that grim line again. "Sometimes I think that's the only way to get through to you."

Val grinned suddenly. "You sound like my brothers."

"They have my sympathy!"

Val turned away. She could feel her eyes beginning to sting. Still, he had been awfully decent about supporting the rally today.

"Look, I'm sorry—"

"Hey, if I said anything—"

They stopped and started to laugh. The tension dissolved.

"You know my big mouth." The wind tousled his hair and he seemed surprisingly vulnerable.

"Not any bigger than mine," Val acknowledged.

"You do speak your mind." He laughed when the color came into her face. "Didn't mean to embarrass you."

"Liar!" she retorted, but didn't really mind his teasing.

"How about calling a truce?" He pulled her down next to him on the stands. "We both want the same thing and fighting each other isn't going to accomplish it."

"I know." Val suddenly felt shy, sitting alone with him on the deserted football field. "You surprised me, you know. Being in the relay."

"What did you think I'd do, picket the field?"

He looked so outraged she couldn't resist teasing him. "How would I know? You could be a sore loser."

He moved fast but Val took off across the field and would have made it if he hadn't brought her down with a swift tackle. In a moment he had her arms pinned.

"You going to take that back?" His eyes laughed at her.

"Is this the way you win arguments?" she panted.

"You'd better believe it." His face was close to hers. "So, what do you say?"

"Okay, okay, you win," she grumbled, but he didn't let her go. For one breathless moment she thought he would kiss her, but then he straightened and pulled her to her feet.

Val was very aware of him as she brushed off her jeans.

Finally Dirk asked, "You really didn't think I'd show?"

Val walked over to the sound equipment and began collecting the tapes. "I guess I don't know you very well."

"Maybe we can remedy that."

She almost dropped the tapes. "What did you have in mind?"

"Maybe getting together before school. You know, so we won't be at cross purposes. How about Monday?"

That was hardly what Val had in mind. "Frankly, I'm never here early enough to do more than grab my books and get to class. But I think we do need to talk," she added hastily before he could get the idea she was brushing him off. "So why not come to my house tomorrow? We can toss some ideas around and you can stay for dinner if you like." Val made her voice as casual as possible but waited tensly for his reply.

"Sounds good." He picked up his backpack. "I work nine to two on Saturdays at Bill's Bike Shop. Three be okay?"

"Fine." she gave him her address.

As they left the field, he checked his watch.

"Ten minutes and no argument. That must be a new record for us."

"Only because you're on your good behavior." She grinned and dumped the tape recorder into his arms before he could retaliate. "See you tomorrow."

"I owe you one," he yelled before turning toward the student council office.

Val couldn't believe it. He was actually coming! She found herself making little running hops and slowed down before she came to class. Her English teacher would not appreciate her disturbing everyone with a noisy entrance.

Although she tried to pay attention to the discussion of Camus' *The Stranger*, Val found her mind wandering. What should she wear tomorrow? Jeans probably, cutoffs maybe. She didn't want to overdo it. Dirk might get the wrong idea if she wore a new dress. Then there was the problem of her brothers. They were not too subtle if they didn't like someone, and she'd complained so much about Dirk that he wasn't too popular with them. She'd better enlist her mother's help to keep them in line.

What she really wanted was some time alone with him. Only to talk over school problems, she told herself, but then had to grin at her own self-deceit.

"Something amusing in Camus, Val?" her teacher inquired, and Dirk's face dissolved into Mrs. Owen's.

"No." She didn't even know what chapter they were on. "Not really."

Mrs. Owen kept an eye on her for the rest of the period and Val had to concentrate on Meursault and his trial. No one was happier than Val to hear the lunch bell, and she hurried to the cafeteria to find Nell. But it was Karen she saw in the lunch line.

"Recovered from the rally?" Karen asked.

Val reached for a Mexican taco. "Chalk it up to experience."

"You have a good attitude." Karen's warm approval made Val feel a bit guilty. What if Karen really cared about Dirk? She wouldn't like the idea of Val's inviting him over tomorrow. But if they were really serious, Val told herself, he wouldn't have agreed to come. Or, even more depressing, he would have because she didn't mean anything to him.

Both girls left the lunch line together and Val asked Karen to join her.

She hesitated. "Don't you usually eat with Nell?"

"Usually," Val admitted. "unless there's a new guy in her life." What she really wanted was a chance to talk to Karen. If anyone knew Dirk, she did.

"Think the kids liked the relay?" Holding the brittle shell carefully, Val bit into her taco.

"The guys enjoyed watching Nell." Karen grinned.

"They always do." She took a sip of soda, hoping to appear casual. "Dirk didn't seem to mind either."

Karen added dressing to her salad. "He's a good sport."

"Have you known him long?" Val hoped she looked like it didn't matter but hung on every word.

"Since freshman year." Karen laughed. "He

used to get me in such trouble by breaking me up in class. I never could get him to stop."

"He does have a mind of his own."

Karen put down her fork and leaned forward. "I know the two of you haven't exactly hit it off, but you have to understand where Dirk's coming from. He's an army brat, you know."

That took Val by surprise. She lost interest in her taco.

"Most of his life he's been on the move, until his father retired." Karen's green eyes grew thoughtful. "I guess security is important to him. That's why he cares so much for Miramar traditions."

That explained a lot, but now she had another problem. How did Karen know so much? She and Dirk must be pretty tight for him to confide in her. Val lost her appetite.

When Nell came in, Val waved her over but she joined some other Winona students eating in the corner.

"I don't think Nell likes me," Karen observed.

"Don't be silly. She probably left her contacts home again and didn't see us. I'll catch her later."

But she missed Nell after school and had to babysit the Fraser twins that night, so had no time to call. Somehow Saturday went by so quickly, Dirk was ringing the bell before she knew it

Ralph beat her to the door. "You must be Dirk." He gave him the once over. "Any good at football?"

"Fair." Dirk was about as tall as Ralph and looked like he could handle himself well.

"My brothers and I are getting up a game. Want to play?" he offered.

Val pushed Ralph out of the way. "Dirk's here to talk school business," she insisted, but had overlooked Dirk's response to any challenge.

"Sure," Dirk said quickly. "Why not?"

But Val was not about to let Dirk slip through her fingers for the rest of the afternoon. "I'm playing too," she announced. "So it'll have to be touch football."

"Better run faster than yesterday then," Dirk teased, reminding her of his tackle on the field.

The color came to Val's face but she laughed. "You just watch me."

Ralph yelled impatiently from the patio. "Come on, you guys. Get the lead out!"

Ignoring him, Val led Dirk to the kitchen to meet her mother, then out to the back lawn where her brothers were already tossing the ball around.

"Remember, you guys," she warned them. "Use your hands only to grasp, pull, or push, not mangle your opponent."

"Would we do that?" Joe's innocent voice was one she'd long ago learned to distrust.

"Frequently." She turned to Dirk. "You gotta watch these guys every minute."

"Don't worry," he grinned. "I may teach them a few things."

"I'll take Val," Ralph declared. "As the superior player, I need a handicap anyway."

"Another remark like that and you'll have a handicap," Val threatened. He responded with exaggerated fear.

"Come on, Dad," Jim yelled. "We need you in the lineup."

After a halfhearted protest, her father got out of the hammock and joined them. He'd been a strong athlete in college and still loved the competition.

Experience had taught Val to play smart, using her natural quickness and good balance, so she handled herself well.

In the huddle, Ralph called a down and in pattern for Val. "Juke Dirk's socks off on this one, okay?"

She nodded. Quarterbacking, he called for the snap with Jim at center and Val his receiver.

"Hut, hut!"

Dirk was covering Val as she ran down the field, but she faked left and cut down to the middle, catching the pass with nothing but daylight between her and the end zone.

"Way to go," Ralph yelled, but Val was watching an obviously embarrassed Dirk return to talk defense with Joe and her father. Maybe her playing hadn't been such a good idea.

Visibly more determined, Dirk blocked the next two passes, forcing Ralph to revise his strategy. He used Jim as receiver until Dirk switched to cover him. Then Ralph told Val to run a crossing pattern, gambling on her ability to outrun Joe, who was covering her.

But as she and Jim ran toward each other to set up the cross, Jim swerved and Dirk crashed head on into Val. She caught the full impact and down she went, while Jim made the pass and went on uncontested.

Dirk bent over her anxiously. "You okay, Val?"

With the wind knocked out of her, she couldn't speak for a moment, but was conscious of his body partly covering hers. Feeling returned in a rush, but she felt no patricular desire to move.

Dirk felt her arms and legs. "No broken bones?"

She smiled up at him. "I don't think so."

"Naw, she's all right." Jim bumped Dirk aside and dragged Val to her feet. "She's survived worse."

"You sure?" The concern in Dirk's voice more than made up for the bruises she'd received.

"Don't worry about Val," Jim assured him with brotherly indifference. "Come on. Let's get on with the game."

"And remember," Ralph added. "The name of the game is 'touch' football. No fair trampling my receivers."

Dirk grinned. "As long as she keeps out of my way."

The game was close, with Ralph managing to pull it off in the last few plays. Walking to the house, he admitted to Val, "Dirk's not bad. You know, you can learn a lot from watching a guy play football."

"Yeah?" She mopped her face with a towel. "So what did you learn about Dirk?"

They both glanced over to where he stood, involved in a heated discussion with her father over whether the Dodgers would win the pennant.

"For starters, he knows how to win and he's no quitter. That makes him okay in my book." Ralph grinned. "I think you're going to have your hands full with him."

Well aware of that already, Val was nevertheless pleased to hear the approval in Ralph's voice. Though she'd never admit it, her brother's opinion meant a lot to her. If Ralph respected Dirk, he was certainly worth pursuing.

Ralph called to him from the patio before going into shower and change for his date. "Good game, Dirk! Come by and we'll play again." He winked at Val and went inside.

"What's the time?" Joe had to be at work by six.

"Nearly five." Her mother handed Val a tray of lemonade. "We'll be barbecuing," she told her, "so why don't you and Dirk just make yourselves comfortable on the swing."

She pointed to a wooden structure half hidden beneath a grape arbor. The September day was still mild and a slight breeze tumbled the green leaves.

Dirk settled himself in the swing. "Now that I've met your brothers, I can see why you're such a good fighter."

Without thinking she retorted, "That's not my only asset." Then she realized what she'd said.

Dirk looked at her figure, outlined by cutoff jeans and a T-shirt. "I'll say."

To cover her confusion, she handed him some lemonade, wishing she wasn't cursed with such fair skin.

Pushing the swing gently with his foot, Dirk continued to tease. "What are our chances of getting through the next council meeting without an argument?"

"What's on the agenda?"

He laughed. "You certainly are cautious."

"That also comes from living with three brothers." She had braided her hair for the game and pulled off the rubber bands, running her fingers through the strands to loosen them. "Karen says you're an army brat. That must have been rough."

The swing stopped and Dirk grew still, as if he had retreated deep within himself.

"Dirk, I didn't mean to pry—" she began, but he stopped her apology with a move of his hand.

"You weren't. It's just, well, some of the memories are not all that great." He made a conscious effort to overcome whatever he still felt. "Besides, it wasn't all bad. I got to see a lot of the country. Even lived in Germany for two years."

Val didn't want him to close up again. "Where did you go to school?"

"On the base. It's not all that different from here except . . ." He hesitated.

"Except what?"

Again she glimpsed the pain. "You never really belong. I mean, after the first two moves I just figured, why bother making new friends? All I ever did was lose them."

"And it hurt."

"Yeah."

Neither of them spoke for a few minutes but his arm lay across the back of the swing and Val was conscious of his fingers touching her shoulder. She moved closer.

"You know, Miramar's the first school I've actually started and will graduate from." He gently set the swing in motion again. "I guess that's why it's so important to me."

Val tried to imagine herself moving from school to school, making new friends, leaving them. What would it have been like without Nell?

"I don't think I could have handled it," she admitted. "All my life I've lived here, gone to the same grammar school, same junior high, and then to Winona till it closed."

He looked envious. "You were lucky."

"After what you've been through, you must have thought my complaints about Winona were pretty dumb." She couldn't look at him.

But his reassurance was quick in coming. "No. It always hurts when you lose something or someone you love."

Dirk reached for her then, touched the black hair that covered her cheek, and leaned closer.

"Ready for dinner, Val? Dirk?" her mother called.

Dirk straightened so abruptly he almost threw them out of the swing.

Why, Val fumed, did they have to eat on time tonight of all nights?

Awkwardly they went to the table and for the rest of the evening Val was forced to watch Jim debate the merits of various colleges with Dirk, and her father quiz him on living in Germany. Sometimes Val envied orphans.

But on Monday she felt quite mellow when she entered the council meeting after school. Having mastered Robert's Rules, Val felt confident and was unprepared for the conflict that erupted over the Inter-Council Tournament.

Nell had the floor. "I spoke to one of the guys at Ramona High and he said they were interested in a volleyball game."

Dirk passed Val the gavel. "May I step out of my role?" he requested formally so he could join the debate. Permission being granted, he responded to Nell. "The reason Ramona wants volleyball is they've got a couple of hotshots over there who'll murder us." He turned to the rest of the group. "What I want to propose instead is softball. We could even use our own field, which would give us an edge." His eyes had that same competitive gleam Val had seen often in her brothers'.

But Nell wasn't about to give up. Regaining the floor, she argued, "Vollyball's much faster moving and more exciting to watch and play. Plus, Ramona's got a great outdoor court." She squinted across the room as if to gauge their reactions before she threw out her final challenge. "Are we going to let a few so-called hotshot players scare us off?"

Val knew Nell's real reason for wanting volleyball, and it wasn't the court or the speed with which the game was played. It was the one sport she could play.

Dirk had the floor again. "No one's scaring us off. But be realistic," he urged. "More kids can play softball, so you get more involvement. Isn't that the whole reason for the tournament?"

Val had to admit he had a point.

Dirk continued, "What we want to do is generate some spirit, get all the kids rooting for Miramar. And the more kids that play, the more spirit."

Responding to a nudge from Nell, Val felt compelled to give her some support. She handed Dirk the gavel and took the floor.

"But the better the game, the better the spirit," she pointed out. "And volleyball's very fast moving. It will get the kids more excited. Get them more involved."

Dirk remained unconvinced. When he regained the floor, he argued, "And those Ramona hotshots will run us right into the ground." Val tried to object but he didn't give her a chance.

"We're really better off with softball. There we're evenly matched."

Val finally managed to regain the floor. "But we don't even know for sure if the Ramona volleyball team is that good. Some of those hotshots may not even be on the student council. And the tournament is limited to council members, right?"

Even Dirk had to admit no other kids could play, but then he brought forth his final argument.

"We've always played softball for the Miramar tournament. It's a tradition."

Val considered that the best argument for change. That attitude was just what was wrong with Miramar—too tradition-bound.

But then she remembered why traditions were so important to Dirk. She thought of the little boy forced to move constantly and leave his friends. Was this issue really that important? After all, softball did give more kids a chance to play.

But as she voted with him to give softball the majority, Val worried that she was letting the Winona kids down. Was she voting in their best interests, or not to hurt Dirk?

Chapter Five

Nell had no such doubts about Val's motives. "You went over to the enemy," she accused. Her hazel eyes had turned stormy gray, and Val knew she was furious.

"Dirk's not the enemy." Val hurried Nell outside before someone heard her.

"No?" Nell stood in the center walk and refused to budge. "Then why is he opposed to every new idea, every suggestion we propose?"

"You have to see it from his point of view," Val urged. Miramar traditions are important to him—"

Nell looked ready to explode. "And Winona traditions aren't important to us?"

"I didn't say that," Val defended herself.

"No," Nell retorted. "Dirk probably did."

"And what's that supposed to mean?" Val was starting to lose her patience.

"You figure it out!"

Nell stalked off, and for a moment Val almost let her go. But then she began wondering if there were any truth in Nell's accusation. Was she becoming one of those girls who lost their own opinions once they had a boyfriend? Val dismissed the idea promptly. Dirk was hardly her boyfriend. He had never even asked her out.

But she had backed down on the volleyball, even though she knew Nell and the other Winonas wanted it. Had she been disloyal?

Val felt pulled in two and didn't like it. She hurried after Nell. Maybe if she explained why she'd voted the way she had, Nell would understand. And maybe Val would, too.

"Wait up!" she called, but Nell didn't stop. Val ran ahead and cut her off. "Are you going to listen or do I call my brothers?"

It was a threat she'd used as a kid and Nell couldn't stop her smile.

"That's better." Val fell into step beside her. "Now lighten up and let's talk about it."

They got into Joe's car and Val drove the few blocks to the beach. The deep green fronds of the palm trees bent in the September breeze like broken windmills above the sky. Val parked near the white hut selling burgers, corn dogs, and thick shakes.

"Shall we?" Val asked.

Nell glanced at her hips and shrugged. "Why not?"

Armed with two strawberry shakes, they kicked off their shoes and sat down on the sand.

Val got right to the point. "So you think I've gone over to the enemy."

"I'm not the only one who thinks so."

Nell's words hurt. "Just because I went along with Dirk?" She swallowed some strawberry shake to ease the constriction in her throat.

Nell shifted and looked uncomfortable. "That and having lunch with Karen."

Val wondered if Nell might be jealous, but decided to tackle one problem at a time. "Look, I voted for softball because more people can play and it didn't seem worth splitting the council over."

"You know the Winona kids on the council are crack volleyball players." Nell still sounded bitter. "You let us down and I still think you did it to impress Dirk."

Val spoke sharply. "Don't be dumb!"

"Then be honest." Nell faced her. "You like him, don't you?"

Val felt like a moth pinned to the wall. "We've never dated."

Nell pounced. "But you'd like to."

"Okay, sure I would. What does that make me?" she demanded. "Benedict Arnold?" With a quick twist of her wrist, she flung her empty container into the nearby bin. Why did everything have to be so complicated?

Her eyes followed a white sailboat cresting each wave. That's what she needed. A boat, so she could sail across the Pacific to Hawaii or Japan and forget all about everything.

But that wasn't really the answer. Not only couldn't she sail, she'd never run away from anything in her life.

Determined to make Nell understand, Val turned to her.

"Look, give him a break. Dirk's had a rough time, too. Did you know he was an army brat who spent most of his life moving from place to place?"

"No wonder he's always giving orders." Nell did not sound impressed.

"You're not giving him a chance."

"Look, he may come on like Mr. Nice Guy to you, but so did Jack the Ripper when he wanted something." Nell became serious. "Just be sure Dirk isn't using you to get your vote."

"He wouldn't do that!" But Val remembered her own doubts when he'd bought her breakfast, doubts that had sent her running to the principal.

"Well, don't say I didn't warn you." A gust of wind flung blonde strands across Nell's face and she anchored her hair with a band.

"I make up my own mind," Val stated. "You should know that by now."

Nell didn't answer and Val knew her friend wasn't convinced. For awhile they sat, both watching the dip and glide of the sea gulls, a flutter of white against the September sky.

Like the gulls, Val's own thoughts swooped from confidence in her judgment to fear that Nell was right. Had Dirk come over on Saturday to get to know her better or to sway her vote? Val thought of the swing. She'd wanted his kiss and that was what worried her. Would her feelings interfere with what was best for Winona?

Val dug her fingers into the sand. She'd never doubted herself this way before, but then she'd never met anyone like Dirk either.

"What about you and Karen?" Nell asked suddenly. "You two getting tight?"

"Why? You've never minded my having other friends before." Val wanted whatever was bothering Nell out in the open.

"We never lost our school before." Nell kept her eyes on the sand sifting through her fingers. "I feel so lost and scared. Like I don't fit in."

Val knew what she meant. She still hadn't gotten used to the campus or the crowds, but she should have remembered how Nell came on strongest when she was hurting most.

"You know you'll always be my best friend."
Val felt awkward saying the words.

"Glad something never changes." Nell's voice
broke.

"Oh, Nell!" Val hugged her, wondering how
she would ever manage without her.

Then Nell brushed the sand off her legs. "We'd
better split. It's getting late."

Val wasn't fooled. Nell never wanted anyone
to see what a softie she was, preferring to hide
behind a confident mask. Still, Val had one more
thing to settle.

"What don't you like about Karen?" she asked
as they walked to the car.

"She's a Miramar preppie, isn't that enough?"
Nell waited while Val unlocked the car door.

"She's nice when you get to know her." Val
pulled on her sandals before getting behind the
wheel.

"Who wants to get to know her?" Nell retorted.

Val closed the door. "At least try."

"If you try voting the Winona way at student
council," Nell bargained.

"I'll vote whatever way I think is right." Catching sight of herself in the rearview mirror, Val
groaned and hunted for a brush to untangle her
hair.

"No problem then."

"But remember, Nell," she warned, "we're not
the Winona Tigers anymore. We're part of Miramar whether we like it or not."

"Never!"

Val started the car, wishing she could make
Nell understand. Refusing to become part of
Miramar would only make things harder. Val
didn't particularly like Miramar either, but they

were stuck there for better or worse. And she believed that if they tried, they could make it better.

What Miramar needed was to open up to new ideas and get more spirit. To that end, Val threw herself into the preparations for the inter-council game.

As student body vice-president, Ray Lazell met with the Ramona council to arrange possible playing dates. Watching him, Val couldn't help comparing him to Dirk. Ray boosted her ego and took her to school activities, but Dirk stimulated her in a way Ray never could. She'd tried to ease off with him, and he seemed content with whatever relationship Val wished. When Ray presented the three possible playing dates, he pushed the first Saturday in October and that was the one Miramar's council chose.

Merrie, the council secretary, had designed and stenciled T-shirts with a wildcat holding a softball in its paws. Dirk insisted they wear them, but it took all Val's persuasion to get Nell into one.

Dirk also organized practice sessions before the game, concentrating on basics, especially hitting. As the weakest player, Nell was catcher, with Dirk pitching, Karen on second base, Tim on first because of his height, and Val on third. Ray, Merrie, Robyn, and Josh covered the outfield.

Gradually the team began to shape up, and Val was optimistic on Saturday morning. Nell was grumpy.

"Why do we have to be here so darned early?" She never opened her eyes before ten on Saturdays, and Dirk's insistence that they meet at eight didn't increase his popularity.

"Pregame warm-up," Val reminded her, lifting the cooler from the car trunk. She and Nell had made pies and potato salad for the pot luck meal later.

"You'd think this was a state tournament," Nell grumbled. She was still complaining later as she hit grounders and fly balls to Tim.

"Less talk, more swing!" he ordered and ducked as the ball whizzed past his head. "Very funny."

"I thought so." Nell grinned, and Val couldn't help laughing. She was incorrigible.

Dirk came over to Val, so keyed up he was hardly able to stand still. "Ready to kill them?"

"Of course." Val was looking forward to the game. Her brothers had played baseball since they were kids and usually drafted her when they had to practice. For her the game brought back good memories of hot summers and green grass.

Dirk frowned as Nell missed a ball. "Hope she gets her act together."

"Softball's not her game." Val looked at him curiously. After all, they weren't professionals. What did he expect?

He expected them to win and didn't hesitate to see that they did. His high-arching, lazy pitches were especially difficult to hit, and he managed to strike the first batter out. The next Ramona hitter popped up over to Val, who was at third.

"I've got it!" she yelled, running to make the catch. Suddenly, Dirk came barreling in front of her. What was he doing?

"I've got it," she repeated but he didn't stop.

Instead he cut her off, almost trampling her as he made the catch.

Val was furious. "You do that again and I'll break your leg!"

His skin turned a dull red. "You could have missed."

"So could you!" she retorted and returned to her position. He had a lot to learn about team sports. She wished her brothers were here to teach him.

Dirk returned to the mound and the next hit went into the outfield. Ray, playing in left, quickly scooped up the ball and fired it to Karen at second. She tagged the Ramona runner as he tried to stretch the hit into a double.

"OUT!"

A cheer went up from the Miramar kids, but Val hardly noticed. She was too upset. Nor did Dirk help when she came up to bat and he started telling her how to hit.

"Remember, be patient. Take the first pitch to see how close the umpire's calling them. Then wait on the next to see if it's good before you swing."

She couldn't believe it. He was not only catching for her, now he was telling her how to hit! She'd been batting balls with her brothers since she was a kid, and what she didn't know about the game hadn't been written yet.

"You want to do it for me?"

The stubborn lines appeared around his mouth. "I want to win."

"So I noticed. Too bad you have to put up with us minor leaguers. Maybe you'd be better off out there on your own without the rest of us to screw things up."

Val stomped up to the batter's box, trying to compose herself. The first pitch arched high. She swung and missed.

"Strike one!"

Val could feel Dirk's eyes on her and was determined not to strike out if it killed her. Somehow the game had turned into a contest between the two of them, and she wasn't about to be the loser.

Knowing the infield was watching her stance to determine which way the ball would go, she made a decision. Val placed her front foot close to the plate in a closed stance and waited. When she saw the Ramona fielders shift to the right side of the field, she switched and quickly hit the next pitch down the left-field line, past the left fielder who have moved too far to the right.

"ATAWAY, VAL!"

"GO FOR IT!"

She made it to first, gambled the outfield still hadn't gotten the ball, and ran for second. Val knew it was going to be close. The second baseman expected her to slide, and swiveling, came around with the tag.

"SAFE!"

Maybe this would show Dirk she knew her softball.

But he didn't give an inch. Going up to bat, he taunted, "Not bad, but watch this. Maybe you'll learn something."

Val wanted to wrap the bat around his neck. But what was even more infuriating, he managed to make good his boast by hitting a triple.

Ray sat next to her on the bench. "What's with you two?"

Val jerked a thumb in Dirk's direction. "Ask our hero."

Wisely, Ray did not pursue it. Both watched anxiously as Nell came up to bat, but as Val feared, she tightened up and missed all three balls.

"STRIKE THREE!"

Val kept Nell away from Dirk till he calmed down, but then the whole team began to play like first graders. Karen muffed a double-play ball, Tim missed an easy pop-up, and even Dirk got tagged for a triple.

Suddenly it was the last inning with a tied score and two outs. Val knew they had to stop Ramona before Miramar batted their last. Nothing like a demoralized team to blow it every time. She'd seen it happen.

The next Ramona batter had hit all ground balls, so Val waited, feet spread, knees bent. He connected and she saw the ball coming down the line. Diving to the right, she stretched to get her glove on the ball. She had it! Up, a quick throw to Tim, and the batter was out.

The Miramar crowd went wild and although Ray later hit the winning run, Val was named most valuable player.

One of the Ramona guys shook a finger at Val. "If you hadn't stopped that ball, we'd have had you."

"Dream on," Nell retorted. When he started to reply, she released her blonde hair from its tight ponytail, depriving him of further speech.

"Where'd you learn to play like that?" One of the Ramona girls asked Val.

The tables had been moved onto the field to

hold the food, and the teams were sitting on the grass eating.

"From my brothers," Val explained.

"You have good reflexes."

"And a big mouth." Dirk stood over her.

She scrambled to her feet. "You had it coming!"

They stood there like two antagonists, and Val wondered what had happened to them. This morning she'd hoped he would ask her for a date. Now they were at each other's throats. Why did he have to be so competitive?

She turned her back on him and piled more potato salad and chicken on her plate without noticing what she was doing. Nell waved her over. She was surrounded by the male members of the Ramona team.

All Val really wanted was to go home and forget the whole game, but that would be too obvious. She managed a smile and settled herself on the grass, wondering where Dirk was. She soon found out.

"Any room?" he inquired, his hands full of food.

"Space next to Val." Rick Evans, from Ramona, was not about to budge from Nell's side.

"Mind, champ?" He looked at Val.

"Stop calling me that!" Her stomach was in knots. She wished he'd go away.

Instead he sat next to her, balancing his plate on his knees. "Can't you take a joke?"

"Sure. If I thought it was a joke."

He didn't answer, but shifted so awkwardly he almost dropped his plate. Val grabbed for it.

"Thanks," he muttered.

Neither of them said anything for awhile. Val pretended interest in what Nell was saying, all the while extremely conscious of Dirk on her left.

He suddenly put down his plate. "Look, Val . . ."

She turned eagerly. "Yes?"

"About this afternoon—"

"Is there room for one more?" Karen smiled down at them.

"Let's have a little squeeze play here." Rick moved closer to Nell.

"Another inch and you're dead," she warned.

Karen sat down between Val and Dirk. "You did some hot pitching out there."

"It was okay." He looked at Val and she wished Karen would go away. He was about to apologize, she knew it, and then Karen had to butt in. What rotten timing!

But Karen seemed oblivious as she rattled on about Dirk's pitching. "I liked the one you sent Rick." She grinned as the tall athlete next to Nell. "Really wiped him out."

"Hey, wait a minute!" Rick objected.

Dirk reminded him, "You sent the ball just where I wanted it."

Val ate in silence but Karen more than made up for it.

"Sorry I blew the double play," she apologized.

"Forget it."

Val couldn't believe Dirk's casual dismissal. If she'd missed that play, she'd never have heard the end of it.

He continued to reassure Karen. "No one makes all the right moves."

Karen certainly was, Val thought, and wondered if it were too soon to leave.

"Any more soda?" Dirk asked.

Val was about to suggest he go find out when Karen leaped to her feet.

"I'll get you some."

"Thanks." When Dirk continued eating, Val wondered if Karen always waited on him. Was that what he wanted from a girl? Someone to pump up his ego, bring him his food? No wonder he'd never asked her for a date.

But he hadn't seemed like that when they'd been alone. She thought of those moments on the swing. He had seemed to like her, even tried to kiss her. But now he leaned closer to Karen, and Val pushed aside her half-eaten food. She wasn't hungry.

What was the use of winning the game if you struck out with the captain? And seeing Dirk leave with Karen, Val knew she had.

Chapter Six

Saturday night, Val brooded. Sunday, she decided to put Dirk out of her mind. And Monday she knew she couldn't. Besides, maybe she'd overreacted. In the heat of the game, people get carried away. It was only natural.

She remembered how she'd fought with her brothers over a basketball shot or football play. Everyone was competitive. Nothing wrong with that. It was perfectly natural among athletes. And Dirk was a good athlete.

Although he was stubborn and hardheaded, he still had a lot going for him. Val especially liked the way his eyes crinkled when he teased her. Not when he was being sarcastic like after the game, but the gentle, almost sexy way he kidded her sometimes. Almost as if he really liked her—or was that just wishful thinking?

She still wondered about Karen—sharp dresser, good legs, and those unusual green eyes. Val stared at her own reflection in the bedroom mirror. Why did blue eyes always seem so watery and washed out? She brushed her hair up. Maybe she should have it cut.

Val put down the brush. This was getting her nowhere. What she needed was some positive thinking. She might as well admit it. What she needed was for Dirk to ask her out! But he hadn't called, and even though she got to school early, he wasn't in the cafeteria. The first time Val spotted him was at the student council meeting after school.

Why did he always have to look so darned good? Seeing him in those tan cords and dark brown shirt, Val felt her legs go weak. She sat down abruptly, knowing she was at a distinct disadvantage when he approached. But then she realized he didn't look too sure of himself either.

"I was wondering where you were." He seemed to have trouble meeting her eyes.

"I've been around."

Dirk started tapping his pencil on the table, and Val wished he would stop. He was making her nervous.

"You played a good game Saturday." He still didn't look at her. "Wasn't sure I mentioned it."

She realized he was trying to apologize. "You're not a bad pitcher yourself."

He sounded gruff. "Sometimes I get carried away . . . you know, try to run the whole show." He attempted a laugh which didn't quite come off.

Val didn't know when she'd liked him better. "We all do that sometimes."

Dirk seemed relieved. "Yeah. I hope I didn't say anything—"

"Forget it. I shot off my mouth too," Val admitted.

"I suppose I should feel lucky to be in one piece," he teased.

Val remembered threatening to break his leg and cringed inwardly. When she dared to look up, she saw his eyes held laughter and something more. Her heart began to jump and she waited for him to speak.

Dirk cleared his throat. "Look, Val, why don't we—"

"What are we waiting for?" Tim checked his watch impatiently. "Let's get this show on the road."

Val could have killed him. If she could find tape wide enough, she'd close that big mouth of his once and for all.

"How about having an off-the-record discussion before the meeting? That way we don't have to bother with all those rules," Nell suggested.

Val nodded. "Good idea."

Ignoring Tim's complaints about wasting time, Dirk led the informal discussion. "Homecoming and nominations for queen are on the agenda today."

"Is it that time already?" Robyn stopped brushing her streaked blonde hair in pretended surprise.

"Don't give me that!" Nell wasn't taken in by her act. It had been instant hatred between them from the moment they'd met. "I heard you're already campaigning."

"Not any harder than you!"

"Can we get back to business?" Dirk demanded.

Val swallowed a laugh at his exasperated expression, and then began to wonder if she would be nominated. A Winona homecoming queen—think of it! Val hadn't realized how far her attention had strayed until Nell nudged her. She caught the end of Dirk's remarks.

". . . usually at Miramar each club nominates

one girl and then the top eight chosen become the homecoming court."

Nell broke in. "At Winona each club used to choose ten girls and then the top sixteen were voted on by the entire senior class."

"What's the use of that?" Robyn objected. "Just sounds like more work to me."

"Let me spell it out for you." Nell didn't bother to hide her sarcasm. "It would give more girls a chance."

Robyn continued to admire herself in her lip-stick mirror. "Afraid you won't get nominated?"

Val jumped in before Nell became violent. "Now that we have such a large student body, maybe we should open up the nominations."

"Let's think about it," Dirk suggested.

"What's there to think about?" She couldn't understand why he was hedging. Changing the nominations was no big deal.

Karen spoke up. "Why don't we decide on homecoming itself and come back to the nominations later?"

"What's to discuss?" Tim looked fed up with all the talk. "They march onto the football field, the band plays, and they crown the queen."

"That's it?" Nell didn't bother to hide her scorn.

"No, that's not it." Dirk sounded defensive. "The girls are in formals, their dads in tuxedos—"

"Do you know how much renting a tux costs?" Val couldn't believe he was serious.

He brushed off her objection. "Nobody minds that."

"They will this year," Nell assured him. "Maybe the Miramar kids are rolling in bucks, but not us."

"Nell's right." Val tried to make Dirk understand. "I know a lot of families who can't afford to shell out money for a tux."

"We never wore tuxes at Winona," Ray added.

Dirk lost his patience. "What did you wear? Jeans and a tie?"

Val hated it when he got sarcastic. "Hardly. The girls always wore dresses but not long ones. And their fathers looked finc in their dark suits."

"No wonder it was a bust," Tim mumbled.

Nell bristled. "Who says!"

"Maybe we'd better start the formal meeting," Karen suggested, and before Val could protest Dirk had handed her the gavel.

Having no choice, she opened the meeting, intending to ask permission to speak, but Dirk beat her to it.

"May I step out of my role?" Receiving permission, he continued persuasively. "Look, I know you people from Winona had your own traditions. And we understand they're important to you."

Val didn't think he understood at all.

"But you're at Miramar now—"

"So we have no say in what's happening." Val couldn't keep still any longer.

He frowned. "You're out of order."

"I don't care." She was sick of his rules and his school. "When we came to Miramar, I was under the impression we'd be treated as equals. That means accepting some of our traditions."

Dirk's voice was quiet, but she could hear the anger. "When you have the floor, I'll listen."

She shoved the gavel into his hand and requested permission to speak. "Look, what's so terrible about trying something different? So you've always nominated one girl per club. So this year you nominate ten. And you've always rented tuxedos. Well, this year half your student body can't afford to." She looked around the table. "Is change all that terrible?"

"It won't be homecoming without formals and tuxes. We've always done it that way," Robyn objected when she had the floor.

"What kind of argument is that?" Val countered when she'd once again received permission to speak. "Just because you've always done it that way doesn't matter."

"It does to us," Tim insisted. Taking the floor, he argued forcibly for keeping Miramar traditions.

Nell fought back for Winona ways. Finally, Dirk called for a vote, and with Josh's help the Miramars won.

Val's fist banged on the table in helpless anger.

Dirk turned to her. "Don't take this personally."

"How else should I take it?" she demanded. "We had a valid argument and you know it. Many of us can't afford formals and tuxedos!" Sometimes he made her so mad.

Robyn suggested sweetly, "Maybe none of you will be in the homecoming court, so you won't have to worry."

"Don't bet on it!" Val retorted. If Nell weren't chosen, the whole senior class needed glasses.

Dirk followed her to the door. "Listen, Val. We have to talk."

She ignored him. Anything she said now would only cause a fight.

Later, seated on the floor of her tower room, Val tossed an apple to Nell as her friend exclaimed indignantly, "Can you believe those guys! Especially that Robyn Willis. I just bet she bleaches her hair!"

"Probably." Val stared at the glass wind chimes that hung by the window. The colorful clown faces usually brightened her mood, but not today.

"Still think you can get them to change?" Nell shifted so her back was against Val's bed. "From where I sit, they're about as flexible as chalk."

Val bit into her apple. "You might be right." She walked to the balcony and watched her mother hose down the patio. "What we need to do is show them how much better Miramar could be with a few changes."

"Good luck." Nell grabbed another apple and began tossing them from hand to hand. "You can't convince a closed mind."

Val spun around. "What about homecoming itself? Remember the time we borrowed all those spotlights and had the girls driven in antique cars?"

Nell shook her head. "Never go at Miramar. Not dignified enough."

"So we think of something else. The main thing is to get the votes."

"Easier said than done." Nell lifted Val's Mexican bedspread to hunt for one of her apples.

"What if we organize?" Val persisted. "You know, like they do at those ad agencies."

Nell sounded dubious. "You mean with slides and stuff?"

"More like drawings, but something they can look at, be impressed by." Val sprawled on her bed, her face set in determined lines. "But most important, we've got to be sure of all the Winona votes."

"Especially Josh's," Nell agreed. "Any ideas?"

The phone rang and she squinted across the room at Val's extension. "Aren't you going to answer?"

Val didn't move. "It's probably for Joe. Since he's been home from college all the calls have been for him."

"When's he go back?"

"Next weekend."

"HEY, VAL! PICK UP!" Jim yelled. "IT'S DIRK."

Nell straightened. "Don't answer. Have Jim say you're out."

But Val was already off the bed. "Don't be silly." She picked up the phone, feeling slightly breathless. "Hi!"

"I wasn't sure if you'd speak to me."

She liked the way his voice sounded on the phone, but hadn't entirely forgotten the meeting. "Winonas don't have closed minds," she said pointedly.

Dirk didn't say anything for so long that Val asked, "Are you still there?"

"Yeah." He hesitated again. "Look, maybe this isn't a good idea."

"What?"

"Going out with me."

She couldn't believe it. "Who's going out with you?"

"You are—I mean, will you?"

Val didn't know what to say. She didn't want to appear too eager, but if she hesitated he might change his mind. "When?"

"Tomorrow night." He sounded more hopeful. "I thought we might play some miniature golf."

Nell was shaking her head frantically. "He only wants to brainwash you. Say no."

"Miniature golf sounds good."

"Sounds bad!" Nell groaned. "Tell the geek to get lost!"

"Will you shut up," Val whispered, her hand over the mouthpiece. "He'll hear you."

"Is something wrong?" Dirk asked.

Val pushed Nell away. "No, just some interference on the line. What time will you pick me up?"

"Around seven?"

"Right. See you tomorrow."

Val barely broke the connection before Nell exploded. "Are you crazy! The guy sticks it to us today and you're off to play miniature golf with him tomorrow." She looked up hopefully. "Unless you plan to hit him with the ball?"

"Assault wasn't what I had in mind." She knew Nell was upset and tried to explain. "I figured it would give us a chance to talk. Maybe I can get him to understand how we feel."

"Only thinking of Winona—tell me about it," Nell mocked.

All Val wanted was to be alone to replay the conversation with Dirk. She still couldn't believe he'd called. What she didn't want to do was argue with Nell and was relieved when her mother called ordering her home. Usually Val had no secrets from her friends, but Nell was so set against Dirk. And sometimes Dirk did make Val furious, but at others . . . she turned her thoughts to what she could possibly wear. If only she had some decent clothes!

"How about knickers and knee socks?" Ralph suggested when he found her the following night staring at her wardrobe spread around the room.

"Don't you have something to do?" Val was in no mood for his smart remarks at her expense.

"Not right now. So I can give you the benefit of my expert opinion." He flopped into her chair as if prepared to stay.

"MOTHER!"

He got to his feet with more speed than grace. "Okay, okay, I'm going. Some people just can't accept advice."

Usually his teasing didn't bother Val, but tonight she was too tense and anxious about the date with Dirk. Once again she stared with discouragement at her clothes. Why hadn't she gone shopping?

Finally, at about two minutes to seven, Val decided on sky-blue slacks with a white blouse. She brushed her hair and held it away from her face with a matching blue band. When Dirk saw her, he didn't say much, but from the warmth in his eyes she knew she'd made the right choice.

Jim walked them to the door. "Sure you want to go out with her?" he asked Dirk. "We could give you a better time here."

Val closed the door, cutting of Ralph's yell, "Last chance!"

"Do they always give you such a hard time?" Dirk grinned.

She nodded. "Real ego boosters."

He opened the car door for her. "You do all right."

The glint in his eye reminded Val of their many skirmishes, and laughing, she scrambled into the car.

As they drove, the street lights tinted the pepper trees silver, making the houses look like white ghosts against the dark night.

"You feeling more comfortable at Miramar now?" The intimacy of the front seat seemed to inhibit him.

"Some," she admitted, trying to relax herself. "At least I've finally stopped getting lost."

"Don't let this get around," he confided, "but after three years I still can't find some rooms."

"It's really part of a plot," she said solemnly. "Architects Anonymous."

Dirk picked up her lead. "A secret society aimed at frustrating the high school student."

She grinned. "And helped by administrators who schedule PE and science back to back." She hated that long run across campus.

"You got it!"

They kidded around all the way to the miniature golf range, which used fairy tales as its theme. Illuminated by colored lights, the tiny moats, dragons, castles, and towers looked almost magical.

Soon she and Dirk were facing their first obstacle. Val noticed he was in fine form. She was out of practice and it took three tries before her ball went through Cinderella's coach.

"You've got to ease up on your swing," Dirk advised. "Here, let me show you." He put his arms around her to demonstrate, but that so unnerved Val she hit the ball right off the course.

Dirk laughed. "Maybe you'd better try it alone."

Embarrassed, Val forced herself to concentrate and eventually hit the ball through Rapunzel's tower. Her natural coordination soon showed and she began to catch up with him. But when they tied, Dirk became more intent, his eyes never leaving the course. And when the windmill moving past the hole stopped his ball, his face grew red with annoyance.

Val tried to joke him out of it. "What's the penalty for the loser?"

"I'm not going to lose."

Some devil made her retort, "You never know."

That did it! With a determined swing, he sent his ball straight through the opening. For the rest of the game Dirk didn't even talk, but played with the concentration of Arnold Palmer.

First amused, then challenged, Val kept up with him till they reached the final hole. For this tricky shot, she had to maneuver the ball up into Sleeping Beauty's castle at just the right speed or it wouldn't go through. Dirk had already finished, and she had one stroke to tie him.

Val swung and the ball almost reached the top when it hesitated and came rolling back to her.

"Guess I blew it," she admitted cheerfully and noticed Dirk's big smile. She wondered if it was relief. "Winning really matters to you, doesn't it?"

He swung his club against his leg. "I guess. Anyway, why bother to play if you don't try to win?"

"For the fun of it."

"Not according to my dad." He stopped by the food stand and she chose a strawberry cone. "Maybe it's his military training."

Val began to understand. "Did he always expect a lot of you?"

Dirk paid for the ice cream. "Yeah, I guess." They sat down on a nearby bench. "He has his heart set on my going to West Point when I graduate."

She almost dropped her cone. "Are you?"

He stared at the colored lights strung across the golf course. "If I don't, he'll think I can't take it. You've heard about plebes at West Point?"

"Who hasn't?"

"So I may go for the first year to show him I can take it and then . . ." He popped the remains of his cone into his mouth.

Val didn't want him to stop. She wanted to know all about him. "Then what?"

"I've always been interested in politics." He picked up his club. "Want a rematch?"

She shook her head. "You know, political science is Ralph's major. Now he's going for his Master's, but last summer he worked on Congressman Hinkley's campaign."

Dirk looked impressed. "Really? I'd like to hear about that."

She waited while he turned in the clubs. "Give Ralph a call, or better still, come by and talk."

"Okay."

They walked toward the exit but Val still found the West Point business troubling. "Can't you talk to your dad?" she burst out. "Make him understand about West Point?"

"You don't know him." Dirk reached for her hand and a hundred balloons exploded inside Val. "He's used to giving orders, not hearing excuses."

She was suddenly fiercely protective. "But it's your life!"

He touched the tip of her nose with his finger. "You'd make a good lawyer."

She grinned. "So my brothers tell me. But I believe in fighting for what I want."

He unlocked the car. "So do I. But this is different."

Dirk changed the sbject once they were on their way, and Val didn't push it. After all it was his life, but what a waste. She'd talk to Ralph and see if he could do anything.

It was still early when they pulled up in front of her house and Val asked, "Want to come in?"

"Wish I could." He sounded like he wanted to. "But I've got an English paper due tomorrow. And I've already had one extension."

"Safford's paper on 'Illogic in *Alice in Wonderland*,'" Val guessed.

"You heard about it."

"The whole school has." Val shook her head. "Can you imagine anyone assigning the same topic to the whole class?"

"Weird."

"She is."

They both laughed and then came the awkward pause. Val swallowed, wondering if he would make his move. Should she wait in the car or would that be too obvious? She reached for the door handle but Dirk stopped her.

"Don't I get a victory kiss?"

"For what?" He must be kidding.

"For beating you at miniature golf." The cocky grin she hated was back.

Val found her romantic mood rapidly evaporating. "Are you saying I owe it to you?"

He wouldn't back down. "In a manner of speaking."

"Forget it!"

"To the victor belongs the spoils," he quoted.

With a quick twist, she was out of the car. "To the woman belongs the choice. Night, Dirk."

But she didn't quite make it to the door. For suddenly she was grabbed, spun around, and held tight. "You know you're one exasperating girl!"

"Me?"

But those were the last words she managed, for her lips were silenced by his, warm firm, and surprisingly gentle. Val felt herself uncurling inside like a leaf in the sun.

Suddenly the door jerked open. "Hey, mom! Val's necking again!"

"JIMMY!" Val screamed as Dirk sprang away.

"Get away from that door," her mother ordered and looked at them both apologetically. "I'm so sorry."

"I'd better be going," Dirk mumbled. She'd never seen him so red. "See you."

Watching the speed with which he took off, Val wondered if she would see him again, and turned toward the house with murder in her heart.

Chapter Seven

When Val didn't see Dirk at school the next day, she figured he was probably working down to the wire on his English paper. But he did show up for the student council meeting.

"Get it done?" she asked.

"Just." He slumped in the chair wearily.

She suddenly wanted to smooth the tired lines from his eyes and couldn't help urging, "Why not skip the meeting and go home?"

He didn't even consider it. "No. If I'm going into politics someday, I'll have to work without sleep. So I might as well get used to it. Thanks for the thought though." His eyes crinkled and a grin appeared. "Jim still alive?"

Val knew he was remembering their kiss. "Barely."

"He deserved whatever he got."

His pointed reply sent the warmth to her cheeks and Val was glad when Nell motioned her over.

"Be right back."

He didn't answer, but she knew he was watching her walk over to Nell.

"Sorry to separate Romeo and Juliet, but Merrie finished the drawings." She handed Val some sheets of paper.

"These are great!" Val was amazed. "How did she get them done so fast?"

"Stayed up half the night."

Val made a victory sign to Merrie, whose heart-shaped face glowed with pleasure.

"But next time," Nell complained, "try to get your brainstorms a little earlier. My mom really got on my case for being on the phone so late."

"Did you convince Josh?"

Nell's dimples appeared. "What do you think?"

"You're fantastic." Val grinned. The idea had come to her after her date with Dirk. Immediately, she'd enlisted Nell's help to alert the Winona kids. She had them behind her now but didn't want to show her hand too soon. This would take careful strategy. For a moment, she wondered how Dirk would react, but then assured herself that he would understand.

When the meeting began, Robyn called for a resolution to have the homecoming court stand under flowered arches on the football field.

"I thought we could have some flowers dyed blue and mix them with white ones," she enthused.

The idea of using the school colors to decorate was a popular one and none of the Winonas objected, for Val had primed them.

"Good," Dirk smiled. "That's settled then." He looked pleased with the way things were going and most of the Miramar kids relaxed. That was just what Val wanted. She requested permission to speak.

"With all the hassle and bitterness over the school closure, we really need to show the community we can work together." Val knew good PR was important to Miramar and used it to her advantage. "We can do this by making our homecoming the best they've ever seen."

"Right!"

"We'll show them!"

Encouraged, she continued. "So what I propose is to open with a spectacular fireworks display. Then have the drill team perform until we climax with the homecoming queen's name spelled out in fireworks across the sky." She passed around Merrie's drawings. "Here's an idea of how it might look."

Merrie had sketches of the court on the field, the drill team forming a crown, and fireworks spelling HOMECOMING QUEEN in the sky.

But the drawings produced no cries of excitement. They were examined silently by the Miramars and then rejected.

"Too expensive!"

"Too gaudy!"

"We're aiming for class."

"Even the British had fireworks for Princess Di's wedding," Nell flared. "If it's classy enough for them, it should be for us."

Dirk took the floor with a grim expression. "We appreciate the work you've done on this." He returned the sketches to Val. "But we don't want to turn homecoming into a carnival." He cut off Val's protest. "What we want is something elegant, something formal. Something we can look back on with pride."

Ridding herself of the gavel, Val argued, "We can feel just as proud of fireworks as we can of flowers or formals. You don't seem to understand—"

"We understand all right," Tim interrupted.

"You're trying to take over, to destroy Miramar traditions!"

"You're out of order." Val had had just about enough of him.

"You don't have the gavel," he retorted.

She grabbed it from Dirk. "I do now."

Quickly Dirk received permission to speak. "Tim has a point. You guys from Winona have fought us on everything. Now you work up your own idea and spring it on us. What are we supposed to think? You obviously don't want to work with us, or you'd have shared your idea right from the start." He gave Val a hurt look.

She wanted to tell him she hadn't even thought of the homecoming idea till after their date, but he didn't give her a chance. He was too wound up, too tired, and out of patience. "What you don't seem to understand is we've been running homecoming this way for years and it's been highly successful."

"We're not trying to destroy anything," Val burst out. "We only want a chance to be part of the school by adding our ideas."

"You don't want to become part of the school," he accused. "You want to change it." For once he forgot Robert's Rules.

"What's wrong with change?" Val demanded.

"Nothing, if there's a reason for it. I don't see one here."

Val suddenly understood. He would never see any reason for changing Miramar, for the school was perfect in his eyes.

He continued. "Besides, the whole community will be watching what we do this year, and we don't want to stir up any more hard feelings."

"And a few fireworks will do that?" Val couldn't keep the disbelief out of her voice.

Dirk was beyond reason. "We like the way we've done things around here. Miramar has a good reputation."

"So?" she goaded.

"So we don't want it becoming another Winona!" Anger harshened his features and his hands gripped the table edge.

"What's wrong with Winona?!" She wished they'd never started this but had gone too far to back down.

"What's right with it?" he shouted back.

"I think you're both out of order," Karen said quietly.

Dirk suddenly seemed to realize what he had done and apologized to the council. Val didn't bother. She just sat stunned. Not only was he blind to his school's imperfections, he had Miramar's prejudice against Winona. How could she fight that?

Without another word, Val got up and walked out, leaving a sudden silence behind her. She didn't even know the outcome of the meeting until Nell came by later.

Perching on the kitchen stool, she nibbled on Val's dinner salad. "Your friend Dirk moved so fast, we hardly knew what hit us." Nell sounded bitter. "One minute he was calling for a vote, and the next, fireworks were out and flowers in. I don't think half the kids knew what they were voting for."

Val stared glumly at the counter. She should have stayed. What kind of a president was she to let her own personal feelings interfere with her job?

Nell seemed to guess what she was thinking. "Look, it wasn't your fault. No one blames you."

"And why should they?" Val's father stood in the doorway, his brown eyes curious.

By the time Val finished explaining, they were ready to eat, and after checking with her mom, Nell joined them.

"What bugs me," she complained, "is they won't even try something new."

"That's because they think they're perfect." Val sighed. If only she could make Dirk understand she wasn't out to destroy Miramar but to make it better. What she wanted was to give it more life, more of the spirit that had made Winona such a great place. She knew the discipline had been looser at Winona and some kids did get away with more than they should, but they didn't live in fear of the principal either. What Winona didn't do was conceal problems, which was not the best PR. So the misconceptions about Winona grew and even Dirk had been misled. But how could she prove to him that he was wrong?

Ralph had the answer. "Why not knock their socks off? Show them a homecoming so spectacular they'll be sorry they didn't think of it themselves."

"How can we?" Val picked up her hamburger. "The council's already voted. We lost, remember?"

"So we surprise them." In her excitement, Nell dropped her fork and Joe jumped to get it. "Thanks." She turned back to Val. "You're co-president. You have the authority."

"Not to go against the whole council," Val protested, but she was starting to be persuaded.

"You wouldn't be," Nell insisted. "The vote was close and once the council saw what could be done, they'd be sure to come around."

Val didn't think it would be all that easy but maybe it was worth a shot. What they needed was a good idea.

"Fireworks are out. They already voted them down."

"So we'll think of something else." Nell looked at Val's brothers. "Hey, you guys, what are you waiting for? Let's hear it with the suggestions!"

Challenged, they outdid themselves. "Hire a rock band. That'll liven it up." Jim was learning to play the drums and set the house vibrating with his accompaniment of rock recordings.

Ralph considered it. "David Bowie's classy. He might do."

"Come on, you guys," Val protested. "We're talking about a high school budget here."

"So maybe he'd donate his time." Jim disliked letting go of an idea, especially one of his own.

"Forget it," Val ordered.

"I know!" Nell exclaimed. "We could have the girls come in on horseback."

Her mother stopped cleaning the table. "What if they can't ride?" she inquired.

"Put them in carriages then. Like in the Rose Parade." Nell closed her eyes. "Can't you just see it? Six Palomino horses pulling the homecoming court in an open carriage."

"That would have to be some big carriage," Jim grinned.

Ralph vetoed the idea. "Tacky."

"You got a better one?" Nell demanded.

"Why not fly them in?" Her father had been following the debate with obvious enjoyment.

Ralph hit the table with his fist. "THAT'S IT! You fly a plane overhead and two guys come out skydiving."

"I love it! I love it!" Nell squealed.

"One with the crown, the other with the cape." Val could see it now. The crowd is watching the sky. The divers appear covered with flares. They descend and crown the queen. What a moment!

"And for the grand finale . . ." Ralph was on a roll. "You have a blimp fly over with the queen's name in red lights. How about that?"

"Awesome," Nell approved, but Val's mind was already coping with the practical details.

She turned to her father. "Could you get us a break on the plane?"

"You really serious about this?" He had obviously intended his suggestion as a joke.

"Why not? That is, if we can swing the money," she amended.

"You've got connections so it won't cost that much," Ralph reminded her and turned to persuade their father. "Why couldn't you fly the plane yourself? Save the pilot's fee."

"Good thinking," Val approved.

"I suppose." Her father still looked dubious. "But—"

Ralph didn't want to hear any objections. "Joe and I could do the skydiving."

"What about me?" Jim protested.

"You haven't been doing it that long." Ralph dismissed him. "Besides," he grinned at Val, "we come cheap."

Val eyed them with suspicion. "How cheap?"

"A dance with each girl on the homecoming

court," Joe suggested and Ralph backed him enthusiastically.

"An introduction," Val bargained. "The rest is up to you."

"No problem." Ralph leaned back in his chair, an expression of satisfaction on his face.

"Let's do it, Val." Nell never had any hesitation once she liked an idea.

Val was tempted. When Dirk saw what homecoming could be, he'd realize what she was trying to do. Talk didn't work, so this time she'd show him.

Her mother cut the chocolate pie. "Will your advisor go along with your idea?"

Val had forgotten about Weymouth. "He'll never buy it. He's Miramar all the way."

"So we don't tell him." Nell rarely let anything stop her once she'd made up her mind.

Val started to object, then stopped and looked at Nell.

"PAT SULLIVAN!" They both screamed.

"Who?" her father asked.

"Assistant activities director." Val started eating her pie with renewed appetite.

"Think he'll go for it?" Jim asked.

"Sure. He graduated from Winona with Joe. He's only working at Miramar part-time while going to college. And," Nell's dimples appeared, "he kinda likes me."

"Who doesn't?" Jim nudged Joe, who pushed him back. A wrestling match erupted which was firmly halted by their mother.

"If you have that much energy, start on the dishes."

Val hardly heard their vehement protests, she was so involved in mentally listing what had to be done before the homecoming date. Nor did she have any doubts until she and Nell stood outside the council office the next afternoon.

"What if he doesn't go for it?" Val was beginning to lose confidence.

Nell fluffed her blonde hair and freshened her lip gloss. "He will."

Crossing her fingers, Val followed Nell into the classroom-turned-office, now filled with desks, paper, duplicating machines, and a few typewriters.

Pat Sullivan, short, with a black beard and glasses, was busy running off flyers for the homecoming nominations. Although Mr. Weymouth was officially in charge, Pat took care of most of the details, including the authorization of funds.

"Can we talk to you?" Nell asked.

"Let me do that." Val took over the ditto machine so he could give his full attention to Nell.

"What's on your mind?" He sat on the desk, polishing his glasses, but Val noticed his eyes seldom left Nell.

"We've got a plan but we need your help," she confided, her dimples much in evidence.

"Shoot."

Nell sat in a nearby chair and crossed her legs. "I suppose you've heard about homecoming."

He replaced his glasses. "Strictly formal. No fireworks."

"Right. So we want to surprise them with a real Winona homecoming."

Val didn't want him to get the wrong idea. "We feel we're being asked to accept all Miramar traditions and give up our own. Talking doesn't seem to get us anywhere, so we decided on a little action."

He shook his head. "I won't be part of a plan to split the campus."

"You won't," Val promised. "We don't want to get revenge or anything."

Nell looked up. "We don't?"

Val glared.

"We don't," Nell sighed.

"All we want," Val explained, "is to show them that what we had at Winona can enrich Miramar."

"Right." Nell took over. "We thought if we surprised them with a really awesome homecoming, they'd be more willing to listen to us in the future."

"I know what you've been up against," he admitted, stroking his beard. "And this might just work. What did you have in mind?"

Elated, they outlined the plane and skydiving plan.

He whistled. "Sounds spectacular all right. And what you want from me is the money."

"You can authorize checks from student body funds, can't you?" Nell asked.

"Within limits."

"My dad's going to see about the plane and the blimp," Val explained. "He's a pilot and can get a good deal."

"Her brothers will do the skydiving for free," Nell added. "So how about it?"

He studied them a minute, then stood up. "Okay, on one condition. You get approval from Mr. Harris."

Val had been afraid he'd say that, but before

she could express her dismay, Nell pushed her out the door.

"I was sure you'd blow it," she explained.

"What's to blow?" Val had never felt more discouraged. "Harris will never go along with our ideas."

Nell faced her. "How do you know until you try?"

"Me? What happened to we?"

"I did my part." Nell sounded virtuous. "I convinced Pat. Now it's up to you."

Before Val could protest, Nell marched her over to Harris' office. "With your silver tongue, it'll be a piece of cake," she encouraged and pushed Val inside.

Behind his desk, Mr. Harris looked as formidable as ever, but before she could lose her nerve, Val blurted out her homecoming plan. Anxiously, she watched him consider it.

He leaned back in his chair. "What I most care about is campus unity." His piercing eyes met hers. "I'm not entirely convinced this is the way to accomplish it, but I'm willing to give it a try."

"You won't be sorry," Val promised and made her escape.

Hurrying to find Nell, she could hardly wait to get their plan underway. When Dirk saw the homecoming they had in mind, he'd realize what the Winonas had to offer. Then there'd be no more fighting in council and maybe more dating in private. Homecoming couldn't come fast enough for Val. Spying Nell, she broke into a run.

Chapter Eight

But Val's problems were not over yet. The next conflict erupted during leadership class. This time it was over which stunts would best brighten homecoming week.

"Three-legged races are dumb!"

Val suspected Nell was objecting more to Tim than to his suggestion.

"Who'd ever go out for that?" she continued, her blonde head held at a challenging angle.

"What about a licorice-eating contest?" Val suggested before Tim could carry the argument further. She was weary of all this dissention.

Tim dismissed her idea. "Too juvenile."

"How would you know?" Nell retorted.

"Time-out!" Mr. Weymouth blew his whistle, one of his favorite ways of getting their attention. It made Val feel like she was in the locker room rather than in leadership class.

"What I propose," he continued, "is we let our two team captains here decide. What do you say?"

Val wanted to say it was the worst idea she'd ever heard but Dirk beat her to it.

"I doubt Val and I could agree on anything." He obviously had not forgiven her for walking out of the council meeting. What she'd planned to do was to keep a low profile till he cooled off. Then she'd let homecoming do the rest.

"So if you two can't get along, let's use it!" Karen's green eyes blazed. "Have a contest."

Dirk looked interested. "What kind of a contest?"

"To see who can come up with the best ideas," she explained. "You do Monday and Wednesday and let Val take care of Tuesday and Thursday. Then on Friday, the kids get to vote on which of you ran the best stunts."

"Big deal. Why should anyone care about that?" Robyn looked bored.

"They will if the loser gets a pie in the face," Tim said slyly.

Val always thought he had a big mouth and now she was sure of it.

Mr. Weymouth smacked his fist into his hand. "Sounds like a field goal to me!"

"I don't know," Val hedged. What she didn't want was more competition with Dirk. "We already have a contest for the queen, why not work together on this?"

"We can't. That's just the point." Dirk sounded as if he blamed her.

"We might if we try." Why was he being so stubborn?

"What's the matter, Robinson?" Dirk challenged. "Afraid you'll lose?"

That did it. "Not me. Better prepare yourself for that pie, Atwood."

"WAY TO GO, VAL!"

"Hey, are you going to stand for that, Dirk?" Tim was on his feet when Mr. Weymouth blew his whistle again.

"Hold it down. I like your fighting spirit, but

we need to get organized. Now I want each of you to pick your team members and get into a huddle. Pat needs the activities list by Wednesday."

"You got it." Dirk chose Karen, Tim, and Robyn for his group, and immediately Val picked Nell, Ray, and Merrie.

"Can we go outside?" Nell asked. "We don't want any eavesdroppers stealing our stuff." She gave Tim a pointed look.

"Don't worry," he assured her. "Whatever you've got in mind, we've already thought of and discarded."

"Come on." Val pulled Nell outside before she could say anything more.

"He makes me so mad." She dumped her books on the grass and dropped down beside them.

"So we noticed." Ray grinned. Merrie waited till he'd settled himself before choosing a spot beside him.

"Okay." A stiff breeze made Val anchor her notebook. "What about the licorice-eating idea?"

"You heard the expert inside." Nell mimicked Tim's voice. "Too juvenile."

Val had a thought. "Okay, so what if we take that idea and use it? You know, for a theme. Act like kids."

Nell caught on immediately. "Dress like kids."

"Braids and lollipops."

"Guys in short pants."

"Somebody write this down!" Merrie dug out some paper from her binder. "Okay, how about licorice-eating on Thursday then?" Val suggested.

"Why not pie eating?" Ray proposed. "That's always good for a laugh."

"Right!" Nell pushed her hair out of her eyes. "With maybe musical chairs for Tuesday."

"Perfect. We can have signs reading: KIDS' DAY: TUESDAY AND THURSDAY!" Val was starting to get excited.

"I'll make the signs," Merrie offered.

Val turned to Ray. "Can you talk to the janitors about the chairs?" He nodded, always ready to help Val. "And try to get the school band," she added. "Live music is always better than tape."

"Not if you're listening to our band," Nell reminded her.

She had a point. "So we hire a rock group."

Ray came to life. "Why not my brother's band? You've been saying you'd give them a chance."

He'd been pushing that band since junior year. "What are they called now?" Val never could keep track. For some reason they changed names as often as they did music.

"Ready for this?" Ray looked proud. "The Hoofbeats."

"We want them to play for musical chairs, not a horse race," Nell informed him.

Val suddenly remembered how much homecoming would cost and decided to stick with their own band. "They come cheap," she explained to Ray.

He looked disappointed. "They have to," he mumbled.

Val quickly changed the subject. "To keep the costs down, let's make the pies for the contest."

"I can do that," Merrie volunteered again.

"Good." She was usually so quiet, Val had never really gotten to know her. But she seemed willing enough.

"So who's handling the prizes?" Nell shifted her position and looked at her watch.

"We are." Val got to her feet. "That about wraps it up. So let's get cracking. Why don't we start with the signs—" She broke off when she saw Dirk watching from the door of the classroom.

The cocky grin was back. "What kind of pie do you like?"

"Doesn't matter. You're the one who'll be wearing it," she retorted.

"Not after what we've planned." He rubbed his hands in anticipation.

Val hoped he was wrong. She didn't relish the thought of a pie in the face, particularly with him doing the throwing. But her brothers had taught her to bluff. "Forget it. You're outclassed and you know it."

"Dream on."

The bell prevented further exchanges and Val hurried off to English, vowing this was one contest she was not going to lose. But as it turned out, Nell was the real winner.

The next week when Val left her government class, Nell grabbed her.

"Want to hear a secret?" She didn't wait for an answer. "I'm one of them!"

"One of what?" Val was going to be late for math unless Nell let go of her arm.

"One of the homecoming court. The spirit club nominated me."

Val forgot all about math. "Fantastic!" She'd kept her own hopes quiet, but was dying to know if she'd been chosen too. "How did you find out? The results won't be announced till lunch."

Nell looked smug. "I've got a friend on the paper. He got me the word early."

"Larry Dunham?" Val knew Nell had been dating him but didn't think it was serious.

"Never reveal my sources." Too excited to stand still, Nell whirled around, knocking into two passing boys.

"Hey, watch it!"

"Lighten up." Nell's dimples turned them into instant slaves. "You may be talking to the next homecoming queen." Suddenly she looked stricken. "Here I am going on and on about myself and you must feel awful." Sympathy softened her hazel eyes. "Are you very disappointed you weren't chosen?"

Val hadn't known she wasn't chosen until Nell's words, but she managed a smile. "Not really." She elbowed her way down the east walk, surprised at how let down she did feel. Pride came to her rescue. "Sure, it would have been great, but I never expected it. Not after Robyn told me the guys in letterman's club considered me too aggressive."

"Those jocks." Nell dismissed the varsity players with a wave of her hand. Then she became indignant. "Why is it that being aggressive is great for a guy but not a girl? Besides, you're no more aggressive than me and I was chosen."

"You have other assets." Val squeezed past the bodies jammed in front of the rest rooms.

"Not any better than yours." No one was more loyal than Nell. "Why, your nose is straighter and you don't have an overbite."

"Somehow I don't think that's what they voted on." Val looked at Nell's curves.

Her dimples appeared. "Anyway, now I have to decide who to go with."

The late bell rang and they both started to run.

"Don't tell me no one's asked you yet?" Val panted.

"Sure they've asked." Nell shifted her books. "I just haven't made up my mind." She sped off to the science wing and Val slid into her seat a half second before Polinsky could mark her absent.

She tried to sort out her feelings. Was she jealous of Nell? Not really, for over the years she'd gotten used to her friend's effect on guys. But she couldn't help being disappointed, and even had to admit she'd imagined her name spelled out in red lights across the sky. VAL ROBINSON—HOMECOMING QUEEN! Now she hadn't even made the court. With a sigh, she opened her math book and tried to concentrate on equations.

But on Monday of homecoming week, her disappointment had turned to pride as Nell took her place with the rest of the court. Not that she didn't still wish she were one of them, especially when she saw Robyn and Karen take their places on the platform set up on the quad.

As Dirk presented their escorts, Val wondered if he were taking Karen. She was relieved when Tim joined the green-eyed girl. Val told herself it didn't matter who Dirk asked, but kept wondering nonetheless.

Larry Dunham, Nell's choice, came up next and Val could see why her friend was attracted to him. He reminded Val of a pirate, all swagger and grin and ready for anything.

Suddenly Val realized that the Miramar guys escorted Miramar girls and the same was true for the Winonas. Socially, the campus was still divided, and Val found that fact disturbing.

"Hey, you guys! Let's hear it for them," Dirk yelled, and some of the kids cheered. The rest just stood around.

He was playing to a hard audience, and Val certainly hoped he'd get them primed before tomorrow when she'd take over.

"Okay, now let me tell you what we have planned." She could tell he was nervous; his voice was louder than usual and sounded forced. "Not just a series of stunts for homecoming week, but a contest. Between me and Val Robinson!" He pointed to where she stood. Val tried not to look self-conscious when the kids turned around.

"On Friday," Dirk explained, "you'll all vote on which of us has organized the best stunts. The loser gets a pie in the kisser."

The response was loud and this time much more enthusiastic. Sadists, Val thought.

But Dirk didn't seem to mind. He was probably too sure of winning even to consider the possibility of getting the pie. Enthusiastically, he continued, "Now to kick off homecoming week, we're going to have a tug-of-war between the homecoming court and their escorts."

Dirk quickly led them to the side field where water had turned the center into mud. Each team grabbed an end of the rope.

"Get Nell in front," ordered Tim. "I want to see her go in first."

"Don't hold your breath," Nell retorted, but took the first-line position opposite him.

"Ready?" Dirk called. "Okay, GO!"

Both sides strained against the rope, bracing their feet on the wet grass.

"Come on you guys! You can do it!"

"PULL, NELL! PULL!"

Her face grew red from exertion and Karen tightened her hold behind but slowly Nell's feet began to slip. She moved closer to the mud.

"Get ready for a bath!" Tim exalted, but for once his big mouth betrayed him. A sharp tug from the girls caught him off balance. His foot slipped and down he went, face first into the mud.

The sudden slack on the rope sent Nell over-backwards and she couldn't get up, she was laughing so hard.

When Val saw Tim go after her, she called a warning but it was too late. He'd already captured and dragged Nell into the mud before she could escape.

Laughing, Dirk declared it a tie.

"No way," Val objected. "The girls won!"

His eyes gleamed. "You saw what happened to Nell." For a minute she thought he would throw her in too.

"You going to play fair or not?" No fool, Val was poised for flight.

Dirk grinned. "Don't I always?"

For a moment defenses dropped and they were back on their old footing. Then Ray shattered it.

"Not bad for an opener, Dirk. But wait till you see what Val here has planned for tomorrow."

The teasing warmth faded from his eyes as he withdrew emotionally from her again. "Nothing I can't top." He sauntered over to join Karen.

"Thanks, Ray," Val muttered, aware of a sudden stinging in her eyes.

"What did I do?" He looked so woebegone, she forced a smile.

"Nothing. Guess I'm a little uptight." He seemed to accept this and she raised her voice to be heard across the field.

"Listen up, everybody," Val yelled. "Tomorrow is Kids' Day. We dress like kids, act like kids, and play like them."

"Another mud fight?" someone yelled.

"No. Musical chairs."

The signs went up, bulletin-board notices encouraged participation, and by Tuesday lunch, Val had doubled Dirk's turnout; she would easily beat his turnout for the tug-of-war which had started the contest Monday. Val let the band quiet the crowd before starting her announcement.

"Okay, you guys," she finally said. "I know you're all up for a game of musical chairs." She grinned at the sailor blouses and painted freckles on the faces before her. Eager volunteers came forward and Ray lined up the chairs.

They still needed two more people and some devil made Val say, "What about our student body president over there?" She pointed to Dirk, who looked like Charlie Brown with his shorts, knee socks, and a bow tie. "Let's hear it if you want him in the game."

"Hey, Dirk!"

"Only if my co-president joins me." His eyes met hers in a brief challenge.

Her braids bounced as Val jumped from the platform. "Wouldn't miss it."

Behind her in line, he tugged on a braid. "Been wanting to do that all day."

Before she could retaliate, the music started.

Marching around the chairs, she was conscious of him close to her. She knew his determination to win, and suddenly her own competitive instincts surfaced. When the music stopped, she lunged for a chair. Next to her sat Dirk, but Ray stood alone.

As the game progressed, Val found herself becoming more and more tense. She would not be eliminated before Dirk. Her efforts paid off and soon it was just the two of them.

The music seemed to go on forever with Dirk circling warily behind her. The sudden silence sent her flying toward the chair and she made it. Only Dirk had gotten there first. She was sitting on his lap!

The kids went wild. "GOOD MOVE, VAL!"

"NICE GOING, DIRK."

Val had never been so embarrassed, especially when Dirk held her prisoner, murmuring, "Are you the prize?"

Val finally wriggled free. "The only prize you're getting is a big fat pie. Right in the face."

He leaned back in the chair, his chin at a jaunty angle. "Don't count on it. The week's not over yet."

He wasn't kidding. The next day he triumphed with a VW cram that was a sensation.

"He must have the whole school here," Nell groaned.

Watching, Val could almost feel that sticky pie already.

But she bounced back Thursday with her pie-eating contest. They had more volunteers than pies, and with their hands behind their backs, the eaters soon had cream everywhere but in their mouths.

"Look at Ray," Merrie giggled. "He's even got it on his eyebrows."

Val was on top of the world. Dirk could never beat this. "What about Tim?" She nudged Nell. "Have you ever seen anyone eat so carefully?"

"We'll see about that." Sneaking behind the unsuspecting Tim, she knocked his face into the pie.

"HEY!"

"You had it coming for the tug-of-war!" she yelled, but made herself scarce afterward.

When Tim accepted the prize, he muttered to Val, "Tell your friend I owe her one."

"I'm sure she'll be paralyzed with fright."

"You know," the smirk was back on his face, "I'm going to enjoy seeing you get the pie tomorrow."

"Don't be so sure it'll be me." But Val wondered herself how the vote would go.

She soon found out. Mr. Weymouth had taken the poll Friday morning and the results were announced at lunch.

"First, I want a hand for Val and Dirk who played a good, offensive game!" Everybody cheered. "And now for the results. Who scored the winning run?" He waited while the band played a fanfare and Val wished he'd get on with it.

"Neither," he announced. "What we have here is a tie!"

"A tie?" Val stared for a moment, then realized what that meant. "Oh, no!"

"Oh, yes!" Mr. Weymouth grinned. "Pies for both of you."

The kids stomped, whistled, and cheered as

she and Dirk were led to two waiting chairs. Ray and Tim did the throwing.

Val was determined to be a good sport but could not really believe it was happening. People only got hit with pies in movies, not in real life! But the chocolate cream pie came toward her and instinctively she closed her eyes. A sticky coldness hit her face and she winced but covered with the remark, "At least it's a kind I like."

Dirk grinned at her. "Do I look like that?"

"Worse."

They both started laughing helplessly as the bell rang ending lunch. Mr. Weymouth tossed over some towels and told them to hit the showers. He promised to give them late passes.

Dirk wiped cream from his face and ears. "I thought you had me beat with that Kids' Day idea."

"What about your VW cram?" Already the pie felt gummy, and she scrubbed at her face. "Where did you get that idea?"

"From my dad. Surprised me too."

"And after all that, we both lose." Val doubted if she'd ever feel the same about chocolate cream pie again.

"Val?"

"Yeah?"

He still had some cream on his nose. "How about we bury our differences?"

That was the best news she'd heard all week. "Suits me."

He tackled the goo in his hair before adding in a gruff voice, "You're probably all set for the dance tonight. I mean, it is the last minute and all."

Ray assumed she was going with him, but he'd never actually asked her. "It is late." She wrestled with her conscience.

"What's what I thought." He turned to go.

Her conscience lost. "Are you asking me to go with you?"

"Yeah."

Val was beginning to think getting a pie in the face was worth it after all. "I'd love to."

"You mean it?" He grabbed her and spun her around. "This is going to be one sensational homecoming!"

Val grinned. He didn't know the half of it. But she merely nodded and thought that even with his hair full of cream and chocolate, he still was the best-looking guy on campus.

Chapter Nine

"You're kidding!" Nell's sudden move ripped the hem from her mother's fingers.

"If you don't stand still, I'll never finish this!" She knelt before her daughter, trying to pin up the rest of her hem.

"Sorry." But it was obvious Nell was more interested in Val's announcement than her own new formal. "You're actually going with Dirk Atwood tonight?"

"What's wrong with that?" She wished Nell wouldn't make her feel so defensive.

"Come on. After all he's done, how can you want to go anywhere with him?"

"I'm sure Val has her reasons," Nell's mother remarked with a warning look to her daughter which was promptly ignored.

"What are they?" Nell demanded. "Insanity and masochism?"

"NELL!" For a little woman, Nell's mother had a powerful voice.

"Okay, okay." She shifted restlessly. "Are you almost finished?"

"Just about." She removed the pins from her mouth and sprang to her feet. A prematurely gray woman, Nell's mother had a wiry, compact body that never seemed to tire. She took a position next to Val and asked, "What do you think?"

Nell modeled her lemon-colored formal, with its draped skirt, and a tight bodice supported by tiny satin straps.

"Will I knock 'em dead?"

"You always do." Val was bursting to tell her she'd been chosen homecoming queen but knew she'd better not. Nell could never keep a secret and no one was supposed to know until tonight. Pat Sullivan had only given Val the news to set up the air show.

"Should I wear my hair up or down?" Nell pushed her wavy curls over her head.

"Down," Val decided. "The crown will look better." Then her eyes flew to Nell's face, afraid she'd given it away after all, but her friend assumed she was kidding.

"Boy, are you ever an optimist."

Nell's mother pointed her toward the bedroom. "You'd better change. I don't want you doing any more damage."

"I was only trying it on," Nell defended herself.

"And you only got your heel caught in the hem, pulling out half the pins!"

"You make me sound like a klutz," Nell complained.

"I know my own daughter. Wait!" she called as Nell started across the room. "On second thought, let me do it." Carefully, she lifted the formal over Nell's head. Carrying it to the bedroom, she called to Val, "Yours is all ready. I'll get it for you." Nell's mother had been a top seamstress before she married and Val knew her family could never afford the kind of gown she could make. But she refused any payment except for material and thread, insisting she liked to keep her hand in.

"Thanks." Val could hardly wait to see Dirk's reaction.

Nell stepped out of her long slip and put on her robe. "I still think Dirk's got some nerve waiting till today to ask you. I mean the dance is tonight. It would have served him right if you'd said no." She motioned Val to follow her to the kitchen. "I thought you were going with Ray."

"So did he." Val still felt guilty about that. And Ray had not been pleased when she told him she'd be going with Dirk.

Nell spied some gingerbread and tossed Val a piece. "He can always take Merrie."

"Is she interested in him?"

"Haven't you noticed? She never lets him out of her sight." Nell waved her gingerbread warningly. "You've got to watch those quiet ones."

But Val wasn't worried. Ray was nice enough, but going out with him was like dating her brothers. And she suspected it was more habit than heart for him too.

Nell's mother returned with Val's formal. "Here you are. Now, do you need anything else?"

"Nope." Val held the formal so it wouldn't trail on the floor. "Is that the time? I've got to run."

"Mustn't keep Dirkie waiting."

Val ignored Nell's sarcasm. She would come around as soon as she got to know him better.

Driving home, the dress spread over the back seat, she hoped he'd like the color. But then she reminded herself, if he asked her out when she was covered with chocolate cream pie, anything she put on would be an improvement. She grinned as she remembered how funny he'd looked and the motorist next to her honked and waved. He thought she was grinning at him, but today she loved the whole world and waved back, laughing.

By six-thirty she was dressed, as Dirk was picking her up early. Unfortunately, her brothers had not yet left for the airport and they invaded her bedroom.

"What do you think?" Joe asked, inspecting her carefully.

Ralph circled Val, giving her his full attention, "Not bad. Not bad at all."

Exasperated, Val ordered them out and then ran to the mirror. Her shoulders looked very white above the strapless blue gown which deepened her eyes to violet. Briefly she wished for Nell's fuller figure, but smiled as she slipped the voile top over her head and fastened the high collar. The transparent material floated over her arms, falling to a point below her waist.

"Elegant," her mother approved when Val went downstairs.

"Is that my daughter?" Her father pretended to be amazed. "The best shortstop the Little League ever saw?"

"That was years ago and you know it!" But Val didn't really mind his teasing. She could tell how proud he was.

The bell rang and Val made herself wait instead of running for the door. When Dirk appeared in a white jacket and blue pants, he fulfilled every fantasy she ever had. Walking shyly to meet him, she felt the soft satin curl around her legs.

He didn't move, just held out a corsage of

white rosebuds, but the look on his face was all Val could have wished.

"Does he talk as well as walk?" Jim inquired.

"Knock it off," Val ordered.

Dirk recovered and handed her the flowers.

"Thanks." Neither of them spoke, too caught up in each other, but Ralph was not hindered by any romantic moment.

"Not bad." He inspected the rosebuds. "Ninety-nine-cent special?"

"No, seconds from the supermarket," Dirk retorted. "Don't you guys have anything better to do?"

"Touchy, touchy."

When Val and Dirk were finally alone, he put the corsage on her wrist.

"I checked out the color with your mother," he admitted.

Val touched the tiny white buds with the tip of her finger. "They're perfect." She looked up. He hesitated. Would he kiss her? The moment became awkward. "Shall we go?"

He didn't seem to know what to do with his hands. "Is this yours?" A blue shawl lay nearby.

She nodded and after placing it around her shoulders, he escorted her to the car. As she bent to tuck in her dress, Val's hair swung across her face and Dirk pushed it back gently. She looked up in surprise, then away when she saw the expression in his eyes.

Dirk straightened and closed her car door before coming around to the driver's side. They covered the first few blocks in silence.

Val wondered if anything was wrong. "You're quiet tonight." She felt keyed up in anticipation and couldn't wait for him to see what she'd planned.

"Better than putting my foot into it." He kept his eyes on the road. "With you, I usually manage to say the wrong thing."

"You're not the only one." Val decided to be honest. "Sometimes I feel you're challenging me. Like I have to prove myself."

He gave her a surprised look, then admitted, "I guess it's the same with me. Usually when I'm not sure of myself, I shoot off my mouth to cover up."

"Really? I guess I was too mad to notice."

"You do have a temper," he agreed.

She bristled. "Only me?"

"Okay, okay," he laughed as he drove into the school parking lot. "But tonight let's have no fights, no challenges, no—"

"Pies." She grinned.

"Definitely no pies." He parked, and opened his door. "Do you know how long it took me to get that goo out of my hair?" Dirk sounded more natural now as he came around to help her out.

"Tell me about it."

He held her for a moment. "You should be part of the homecoming court. They must be blind."

A lovely warmth stole through Val. "But then my father would be with us."

"Forget I mentioned it."

But as he led her toward the field, Val knew she never would. Some words were like keepsakes, to be treasured forever.

When they reached the stands reserved for the homecoming court and their escorts, she saw Nell.

Her blonde hair swept her shoulders, reminding Val of a fairy-tale princess. She would make a marvelous homecoming queen. Next to her, Robyn was acting as if she already wore the crown. Wouldn't she be surprised!

On the football field the captains met for the toss. Santa Rosa called it and Miramar won. The players took their positions, but Val had trouble concentrating on the game. Anticipation made it hard to sit still.

"Cold?" Dirk moved closer.

"No. Just excited."

Then Miramar scored. Dirk was on his feet, outshouting the cheerleaders who yelled their approval. Val checked her watch, and when Nell saw her, she winked. Not too much longer.

Finally came the halftime gun. The flower arches were set in position and the band began to play, "Sunshine on My Shoulder." This was it!

On the PA system, Mr. Weymouth announced, "Tonight, the sky's the limit. We pay tribute to the sun, the moon, and the stars . . . not the least of which are our homecoming court."

Val had written his speech, not wanting it filled with football terms. Nell had primed the drill team.

Dirk's arm covered Val's shoulder and he pulled her toward him in an excited hug. "It's looking good."

Val smiled. He hadn't seen anything yet.

When the drill team marched on the field, the lights picked up the gold and silver stars covering their uniforms. Keeping to the music, they formed a sun with rays continually extending. The crowd applauded enthusiastically.

When the band swung into "Harvest Moon," Val's hands began to sweat. It was almost time. Finally the drill team finished with a star pattern to the tune of "Star Baby."

More applause until they regrouped to form a corridor for the homecoming court. Val felt especially proud of Nell as she and her father took their places beneath the flowered arch. Only the queen's platform remained empty. The principal waited.

Dirk frowned. "Where's the crown and cape?"

Val pointed upward. "It's coming!"

Suddenly two skydivers, their bodies covered with flares, appeared. A gasp went up from the stands.

"What's going on?" Dirk demanded.

Red lights appeared on the blimp, spelling CONGRATULATIONS TO OUR QUEEN NELL SIRENCI. Immediately the band blew the trumpets. By now Joe and Ralph had landed and waited with crown and cape while Nell's father escorted her to the queen's platform. There the crown was placed on her head.

Val applauded harder than anybody. The tiny tiara glittered in Nell's blonde hair and the red velvet cape swirled about as she waved. In her other arm, she carried a huge bouquet of red roses.

"Doesn't she look beautiful?" Val gripped Dirk's arm to share the moment and looked surprised when he pulled away.

"Those are your brothers out there, aren't they?" He didn't look pleased. "And that was your father in the plane."

"Sure." She didn't understand why he was

acting so strange. "We had it all planned. I knew when you saw it you'd realize—"

"What a fool you've made of me!"

"No! What are you saying?" Val didn't understand what had gone wrong.

Halftime was ending but Dirk seemed in no mood to watch the game.

"We have to talk." He grabbed her hand and pulled her behind the stands. "You have your nerve going behind my back and arranging for this—this spectacle!"

"Mr. Harris approved the idea," she defended herself, "and you heard the audience. They loved it. Come on, admit it's the best homecoming you've ever seen."

"That's not the point!" He was yelling now. "Why didn't you tell me?"

"Because you wouldn't have gone along! Nothing I said would have convinced you, so I figured we had to show you."

It all seemed so simple to her, but he didn't buy it. "What you mean is I would have stopped you."

"I suppose so, yes," she admitted. "But now that you've seen it, can't you admit you were wrong? That a flashy homecoming is just exactly what the school needed?"

He wouldn't admit anything. "How did you get the money?" Dirk demanded. "Forge the checks?"

That stung. "I'd never do that!"

"Nothing would surprise me anymore." His sarcasm grew more marked.

Val faced him. "What have I done that's so terrible? Just put together one of the best homecomings you'll ever know!"

"We voted on what we wanted and you lost," he pointed out. "But could you handle that? Oh, no. You had to do it your way."

"Not my way exactly." Why did he always have to be so stubborn? "Nell suggested—"

"So Nell's in on it too!" He exploded. "Does the whole student body know? Am I the only one kept in the dark?"

"Stop making it sound like some sort of conspiracy!" Val's own temper was on the rise. "Look, we felt we weren't getting a fair shake. None of you would even listen to anything new, much less try it. So we figured we'd show you. And we were right. You heard the crowd."

"Hey, you two. No necking behind the stands." Val's brothers stood there grinning.

"That's the last thing I had in mind," Dirk retorted and walked off.

"THAT MAKES TWO OF US!" Val ripped off her corsage and threw it after him.

Ralph picked it up, trying to smooth out the crushed petals. "He didn't like it?"

Val raged. "He is the most narrow-minded, stubborn, pigheaded—"

Ralph and Joe exchanged glances. "He didn't like it." They waited while Val tried to compose herself.

Finally, Ralph snapped the corsage back on her wrist, and putting a brotherly arm around her shoulders said confidently, "He'll get over it."

"Maybe he will, but I won't!" She would never forget the way he'd looked at her. As if he hated her.

"Let's watch the game," Joe suggested.

Val went with them, but she couldn't recall

who scored, who fumbled or even who won. How could Dirk turn on her like that? He sounded like she'd planned to make a fool of him. Not that she needed to work very hard to manage that. He did quite well on his own.

Nell was right. She never should have agreed to go to the dance with him. The dance! If he thought she was going out on the floor with him, he was sadly mistaken.

But Val had no choice. No sooner had she introduced her brothers to the homecoming court as promised, than Mr. Weymouth announced, "Our queen and her escort will open the dance, followed by our two student body presidents."

Val wanted to run and hide, but Dirk didn't give her a chance. Grimly, he took her into his arms, forcing her into step. She resisted his lead and they stumbled.

"Loosen up, will you?" He pushed her harder.

"I will if you learn to lead." She fought him every inch of the way.

Nell squinted in their direction as Tim called, "Hey, Dirk and Val? Relax! You're dancing, not arm wrestling."

Dirk yanked her closer and practically carried her around.

She pushed him away. "Do that again and I'll walk off the floor."

He held her tighter. "Try it."

She would have but the music stopped.

Dirk backed away as if she were contagious. "It's been memorable."

"Good. Don't ask for a repeat." She was close to tears but wouldn't show it.

"Not until you learn to dance," he countered and left her.

Val tried to lose herself in the crowd but Nell found her.

"What's with you two?" Her hazel eyes were curious. "You looked like World War Three out there."

"He didn't like the homecoming." Val began to tremble. "He was furious."

"So who cares?" Nell sent Larry to get some soda. "Don't let him spoil your evening. He's not worth it."

"You're right." Val pulled herself together and managed a smile. Somehow she got through the evening, but it did seem endless. Why did she have to fall for someone who not only hated her, but her old school as well? She watched Dirk dance with every girl in the room. Everyone but her. Not that she lacked partners, although most of the guys wanted to know what was going on. Val managed to put them off with a joke, but knew she couldn't take much more.

She went up to Ralph. "Will you take me home?"

He'd been flirting with Robyn but one look at Val's face brought him to her side. "What happened now? Has Dirk done anything?" He looked ready to take him on right there and then.

"No," she assured him hastily. "I just want to leave."

When the tears spilled over, he quickly signaled to Joe. At the door Val took one last look at what she had thought would be the best night of her life. On the dance floor, the girls' pastel dresses swirled like spinning flowers, but Val felt as crushed as the corsage on her wrist.

Chapter Ten

October gave way to November but Dirk still avoided Val. At meetings she felt invisible. Naturally, she pretended she couldn't care less, but the strain was beginning to show. Even Nell noticed.

"You look awful!" Her lunch tray clattered to the table. "And that salad wouldn't keep a rabbit alive." Nell pushed a sandwich across the table. "Here, take this."

Val stared at the ham and cheese but didn't even bother to pick it up. She hadn't been hungry for weeks. Even her mother's fettuccine didn't appeal. And although she knew she was losing weight, she didn't seem to care.

Nell sighed. "It's still Dirk, isn't it?"

Val nodded, keeping her eyes on her plate. She would not cry again.

"That's what I was afraid of." Nell sounded as if she were ready to take him on herself.

Alarmed, Val looked up but Nell was only squinting across the cafeteria.

"Did you leave your contacts home again?" Val demanded.

Nell impatiently brushed aside the question. "Is Dirk here now?"

"Behind you." Val seemed to have radar where

he was concerned. "With Karen," she added gloomily.

Nell squinted in their direction. "He's been hanging around with her a lot lately."

"I know." Val had been forced to watch them together at council meetings and knew they were probably dating.

Nell returned her attention to her toasted cheese sandwich. "Just goes to prove what I said."

"About what?"

"About Miramar students. They stick together." She took a sip of lemonade. "When Dirk found he couldn't push you around, he dropped you."

Val didn't want to believe her, but he'd certainly taken the homecoming personally. Didn't he realize she'd raised the spirit of the school? No one had talked of anything else for weeks afterwards. Didn't that prove Winona ideas could help Miramar? Obviously not to Dirk. He seemed determined to believe she had kept silent about her plans for homecoming to make a fool out of him. Why should he take it so personally?

She wondered if Nell could be right. If he'd dated her just to swing her vote, he'd naturally assume she'd be equally devious. But he'd never tried to influence her on a date, a point she vehemently made to Nell.

"He never had the chance," Nell commented. "You only dated him twice."

That was not what Val wanted to hear. "So what do I do now?"

"Forget him."

"Easy for you to say," Val exploded. "You're not his co-president!"

"Take it easy." Nell pulled her chair closer so

the boy behind her could get out. "Look, I know you're hurting, but what else can you do? Going around moping and crying won't change anything."

Val couldn't deny that, but stared morosely across the cafeteria at Karen who was laughing at something Dirk had said.

Nell jabbed her straw into the crushed ice of her drink. "When I've been burned by a guy, I get my mind on something else."

"Yeah, like another guy," Val retorted.

Nell laughed. "At least you haven't lost your sense of humor."

"Sometimes I wonder." She knew she'd been impossible to live with the last few weeks. Right now Jim wasn't even speaking to her and Ralph had pasted a sign on her door which read: CAUTION! COMBAT ZONE. "My family's ready to ship me out," she admitted.

"Don't worry. You can always move in with me."

That drew a faint smile from Val because Nell already bunked with her younger sister, Jamie, to both their disgust. The only available space was the back porch.

Nell pushed aside the empty plates. "What you need is a new project," she decided. "And I've got just the one. The Christmas dance."

Val dreaded the thought of another dance. "Is it that time already?"

"The stores are decorated, Thanksgiving's next week, and I've already received my first Christmas card. Where have you been?" Nell shook her head in exasperation. "Now, we've got to get moving on the dance. No doubt Weymouth will bring it up tomorrow in leadership class, so what we need is a new and different idea."

"You said that about homecoming," Val reminded her.

"Forget homecoming."

"I wish I could." Val watched Dirk leave with Karen.

"You will if you try. Now pay attention!" Nell tapped her spoon on the table. "You come up with the idea and I'll prime the kids. This time we'll discuss it in class so everything's above board and no one can accuse us of working behind anyone's back."

Val knew she meant Dirk. He'd probably take Karen to the Christmas dance and Val would be lucky if Ray even asked her—particularly after the way she'd treated him over homecoming. Who wanted to plan a dance she wouldn't even attend?

But she knew she couldn't let her friends down, and lying in bed that night, she gave it a try. What they needed was some way to get the kids enthused and unified. But what? Just on the edge of sleep, the idea came to her. Wait till Nell hears this! And that was her last thought before morning.

Feeling better than she had in weeks, Val did not dread leadership class and seeing Dirk. The spring was back in her step and she wore a new blue sweater.

Nell approved. "Much better. Today you look like a person instead of a walking corpse."

"You do say the nicest things." Val sat next to her, for Mr. Weymouth never bothered with seating charts.

Nell jumped to the right conclusion. "You came up with an idea!"

Val nodded as the bell rang. "No time to explain now," she whispered. "Just follow my lead."

"I'll alert the others." By a system known only to Nell and the CIA, she signaled the other Winonas to back Val.

Meanwhile, Mr. Weymouth settled himself on the edge of his desk and smiled in his jovial way. "So, let's get the ball in motion." He directed his question at Dirk. "What's the game plan for the Christmas dance?"

It annoyed Val that he always turned to Dirk first, but to avoid conflict she kept her mouth shut. Ironically, so did Dirk. Since he obviously hadn't been listening, Karen answered for him.

"We've been trying to decide on a theme," she began and Val wondered if they'd been working together. Her insides puckered as if she'd sucked something sour and she wondered if she were going to be sick. Was this what jealousy was like?

Karen continued to hold the floor. "Once we've got the theme, we can work on designing posters and choosing the decorations."

"What about 'Winter Wonderland'?" Robyn suggested. "We could have posters with an old-fashioned sleigh filled with people."

"Or presents." Karen obviously liked the idea. "Then we could decorate the gym with snowflakes and icicles."

"Why not try something different?" Val suggested, for that type of approach had been used in the past. "How about a 'Holiday Hop'?"

"Sounds like Easter," Tim objected.

"Besides," Robyn said, tossing her head to

show off her long hair, "we'll all be in formals. Who wants to hop?" That drew laughs from some of the Miramar kids but only made Val more determined.

"Who wants to wear formals?" she countered.

"We always do."

"But we went that route for homecoming," Val pointed out, aware of the frozen look on Dirk's face. "This time let's try something new."

"Another air show?" Dirk did not bother to hide his sarcasm.

"Not unless you're thinking of flying in Santa Claus," she retorted.

He didn't crack a smile.

Val went on. "What I thought we could do was run a dance contest."

"Sounds good." Ray was half out of his seat. "And I know just the band!"

Tim laughed. "Can't you just see the poster? 'Hop Along with the Hoofbeats!' "

Ray did not laugh. "They've changed their name." He had no sense of humor about his brother's band.

"To what?"

Val knew Tim was setting Ray up. Tim hoped that the new name would be even funnier, and from past experience Val was afraid he might be right. But Ray fooled them all.

"Silverwind."

The kids looked impressed and Ray looked proud. "Merrie thought of it."

Nell nudged her but Val was glad for Ray. Still, she would miss him.

"They know all types of music and would be great for the contest," Ray enthused.

"And each couple would wear a number." Nell

quickly continued to keep the momentum going. "With the winner receiving—"

"A trophy," Merrie finished.

"Not so fast." Dirk held up his hand. "We haven't even decided to go with the dance contest yet."

"Why not?" Val would fight this battle openly. He'd have no chance to accuse her of going behind his back.

Dirk looked annoyed. "You know why not. We've always—"

"Done it that way at Miramar," Val mocked.

Most of the Winona kids laughed. Those from Miramar didn't think it was so funny.

"Sneering at our traditions isn't going to change our minds," Dirk retorted.

"Can anything?"

He didn't like that. "We're not against the idea of a dance contest, just about the timing. How about having it at the Backwards Dance in February?"

"Or the Easter Hop?" Tim smirked.

"Why not the Christmas dance?" Val had heard no good reason to back down. "I think we need to have the kids mingle more." She referred to the pairing at homecoming. None of the Winonas had dated the Miramars.

"So you have them compete in a dance contest." Now it was Dirk's turn to mock. "Nothing like a little competition to foster unity."

"So who says it has to be Winonas against Miramars?" Val didn't want to break apart the school any more than he did. All the Winonas wanted was to belong. "The best dancers would compete. And when you share something, it breaks down barriers. It brings you close."

She was urging him to remember their shared experience with the pies. It had brought them close. Now, he was with her for a moment, his eyes wistful as if he wished they could go back to that day.

But then Tim spoiled it all by opening his big mouth. "You're not buying that argument, are you, Dirk?"

She knew she'd lost then. He'd been put on the spot and couldn't back down now.

"No. I say we go with 'Winter Wonderland.' A formal dance like we always have."

"I say we don't." Val hurt so much inside, she could barely get the words out. Nell looked at her in concern.

"Time out!" Mr. Weymouth blew his whistle. "Let's take an informal vote to see where we all stand."

Val stood and faced the group. "Raise your hand if you want 'Winter Wonderland,' a formal dance."

All the Miramar students put up their hands led by Dirk, Karen, Tim, and Robyn.

"Okay, what about the 'Holiday Hop,' a dance contest?" Now it was Winona unity with Nell, Ray, and Merrie solidly behind her.

"Looks like we're split right down the middle." Mr. Weymouth did not look happy. "I'd advise you to rethink your positions before the council meeting on Friday. If you people can't get together, what can you expect from the rest of the kids?"

The bell rang. Val turned to leave but Dirk blocked her way. "I hope you realize what you're doing."

"I'm just trying to inject a little spirit into

this school." She knew Nell was waiting and tried to get around him.

"Really? I thought you were tearing it apart."

His taunt stopped her. "That's not what I want and you know it."

"But that's what you're going to get." His look was accusing. "I know you primed the vote."

She bristled. "Just because Josh voted with us for a change, and was loyal to—"

"Loyal to what?" he demanded. "Winona's closed. Can't you face that?"

"I have. But have you faced the fact that Miramar's not the perfect school either? That it could benefit from a few new ideas?"

He hit the door with his fist. "Like what? In-school fighting? Didn't you hear what Weymouth just said? If the council is split, the campus will be too. As soon as this gets around, the kids will take sides."

"It won't get around." Val would be late for English if she didn't hurry. She tried to get by but he wasn't through.

"What if we have 'Winter Wonderland' only . . ." He held up his hand as she started to object. "Listen a minute, will you? What if we use the 'Winter Wonderland' idea only with informal dress?"

She recognized his concession but it was too late. Too late for them and too late for compromise. "No. We've always had to give in. Now it's your turn."

"And if we don't?" he demanded. "What'll you do? Arrange another little surprise?"

He would never let her forget homcoming. "No matter what you think, I never meant to hurt you," she said quietly. "And," Val couldn't resist adding, "it was successful."

"I never said it wasn't. I just don't like your methods."

"Why don't you admit it? You don't like anything about me!" Val didn't know what made her say that but all of a sudden something burst inside her.

Dirk looked taken aback. "That's not true. I did . . . I do like you."

"But?" She knew he was holding back.

"But you don't seem to understand how I felt when people congratulated me on keeping the air show such a surprise."

"So that's it." She was amazed she hadn't realized it before. "Your pride was hurt."

"That's not it at all!" he yelled.

The bell rang. "I've got to go."

"Wait!" He touched her arm but she jerked away. His face reddened. "Will you change your vote?"

"No."

"Why must you be so stubborn?" he exploded. "Open your eyes. Look around the campus. Don't you see what's happening?"

Val didn't answer, just started running toward her English class. She felt confused, angry, hurt. Why was she always the stubborn one? It wouldn't kill him to let one of his precious Miramar traditions go.

By the time she got to English she was late again and received detention, but didn't really care. What she needed was to talk to someone, not look for synonyms. The practice SAT defeated her, the time dragged, and she was sure the clock had stopped by the time the bell rang.

She practically ran to the cafeteria and was so eager to talk to Nell, she cut right into the food line.

"Do you think Weymouth's right? That we will split the campus?" The words tumbled out and Nell looked at her in surprise. Behind them two girls grumbled about line jumping but Val ignored them.

"Over whether we have a contest or formal dance?" Nell shook her head. "Don't be crazy."

Val badly needed reassurance. "Dirk said if word got around, the kids would be taking sides."

"Would they?" Nell looked thoughtful. "But they'd need to be revved up first."

Val's mind was on Friday's meeting. "How do you think the vote will go?"

Nell answered absently; she seemed preoccupied suddenly. "They'll win. Josh will fold or Weymouth will break the tie." She thrust her tray into Val's hands. "Look, I almost forgot. I promised to meet Larry. See you after school."

"Nell, wait!" Val called. "I need to talk."

"Later. Trust me, this is important. To all of us." And she was gone.

Val felt abandoned. "Some friend," she muttered and left the tray on the counter. No longer did she have any interest in food. Nor did it help when Nell didn't show after school. Val decided not to wait. Let Larry drive her home!

The rest of the week limped along. Wednesday, Val failed a math test. Thursday, she blew a volleyball game. And Friday didn't hold much promise either, not with the student council meeting scheduled for three o'clock sharp. But the blow fell long before then. At noon when the paper came out, Val stared at the headlines in horror:

POLL SHOWS CAMPUS DIVIDED OVER
CHRISTMAS DANCE!
WINONAS FIGHT MIRAMARS FOR DANCE
CONTEST

Val could not believe what she was reading. When had the poll been taken? She didn't remember hearing anything. But then, she hadn't been paying much attention these last few days.

The article explained that the results of the poll indicated the campus was split, Winonas against the Miramars. After two months, no unity had occurred. Instead, the rift was widening.

This was awful. The whole campus would be involved now. Who had told the paper . . . Nell. She was dating Larry and he was on the staff. Suddenly Val remembered how Nell had dashed off at lunch, and she'd made herself pretty scarce since.

Wait till she got her hands on Nell, Val thought, but turning, came face to face with Dirk. One look at his expression told all. He thought she'd done it.

What could she say to him? She needn't have worried, for he didn't give her a chance to speak. With a look of contempt, he strode past, and Val knew nothing would convince him of her innocence. He believed she'd do anything to sway the council vote—even divide the school.

Chapter Eleven

Anger sent her hunting for Nell. She tracked her down on the west lawn and waved the newspaper under her nose.

"This was your idea, wasn't it?"

Nell jumped to her feet. "Isn't it great! We really had to work fast. Larry and I conducted the informal poll but the results were obvious."

Val could just imagine how objective they'd been.

"With this publicity, the Miramars will have no choice. The dance contest is in!"

Val couldn't believe her ears. Didn't Nell realize what she'd done? But she rambled on, oblivious to Val's silence. "I mean they set themselves up as this big-hearted, welcoming school. So if they back down now, they'll be shown up as the narrow-minded snobs they are!"

"Why didn't you tell me?" Val demanded.

Nell looked a bit uncomfortable. "You would have gotten all paranoid. I mean the way you feel about Dirk and all. Now you're in the clear."

"HE THINKS I DID IT!" Val yelled.

"Relax." Nell stretched out once more on the grass and found an apple in her lunch sack. "I'll set him straight. But I thought it was all over between you two anyway."

"It is now." She would never forgive Nell for this.

Something of what she felt must have shown on her face, for Nell looked uncertain. She sat up as if about to speak when Ray and Merrie joined them.

"Why didn't you mention my brother's band in the paper?" he demanded of Val. "You know they could use the publicity."

"It wasn't Val's idea, it was mine," Nell said quickly, avoiding Val's eyes.

"Okay." Ray was not about to be sidetracked. "But what about Silverwind?"

"Who cares about Silverwind!" Val's patience was at an end. Here the whole campus was taking sides, her world was crumbling, and all he cared about was his brother's band. "Right now we don't even know if there'll be a dance contest."

"You don't have to shout." Merrie looked like an angry sparrow defending a Saint Bernard. "And you know as well as we do that once the pressure's on, the Miramars will fold."

"Serves them right too." Ray glared at Val as if she were one of them.

Val felt suddenly sick. Was everyone out for revenge? Maybe Dirk was right. Maybe she had split the campus.

Nell lifted her long hair from her neck. "Boy is it hot. Maybe we should get out of the sun."

"Hotter inside. I hear it's close to a hundred degrees." Ray took a long drink of soda.

Maybe it was the desert wind, the Santa Ana, that was making everyone so irritable. Val clutched at the idea like a dying man, not wanting to believe she had split the campus. Hadn't she read an article about desert conditions once? Something about negative ions . . .

Karen joined their group. She looked upset. "We have to talk."

Before Val could respond, Nell motioned Ray and Merrie to sit down next to her. "Sorry, no room."

Val was shocked. "Don't be dumb! Of course there's . . ." But Karen was already halfway across the lawn.

"What's the matter with you guys!" Val couldn't take much more. The heat, the guilt, the arguing was all getting to her.

"Let her go," Ray advised. "She's the enemy."

Val didn't waste time arguing but hurried after Karen. She found her on the steps with Robyn and Dirk, but then hesitated. He'd hardly welcome her now, especially after what Nell had done to Karen.

Frustrated, Val turned away and stared at the baking campus beneath the Santa Ynez mountains. Kids in shorts sat on the lawn or at the outdoor tables, and gradually Val became aware of the tension. All the Winona kids ate together. No one mixed. What's more, they were wearing bright yellow T-shirts with black tigers on them. Winona Tigers.

A husky Miramar guy taunted, "Hey, Tigers! Want to get your nails clipped?"

Immediately a Winona kid was on his feet. "Whenever you're ready, big mouth."

Val knew what was going to happen, but she was powerless to stop it. The Miramar guy moved in and soon fists were flying. The kids pushed Val forward as they crowded around. Frightened, she looked for an administrator. None were in sight.

"Get him, Hank!"

"Show him some skin!"

Val began to panic. The heat, the kids, the blood all came in on her. Then she saw Dirk. He'd fought through the crowd and was trying to pull the guys apart.

"Cut it out," he ordered. "This won't solve anything." He grabbed the arm of the husky Miramar football player.

"Hank, you'll get yourself kicked off the team."

But Hank was beyond reason. "Get lost, At-wood." He shook off Dirk's hand and swung wildly, hitting another Winona kid who was watching.

"What do you think you're doing?" Immediately, he retaliated.

"KNOCK IT OFF!" Dirk yelled, but no one paid any attention. The crowd pushed closer, cheering them on. Dirk threw himself between the fighters, trying to separate them, but a sudden swing took him unawares. He went down.

"Dirk!" Val fought to get to him, pushing kids out of the way. More guys were fighting now. The whole quad seemed full of punching, rolling bodies. She had to get to Dirk.

"Let me through!"

"Watch out!"

"Stop pushing!"

A shove sent her to her knees and she put out her hands to protect herself.

"ENOUGH! STOP THIS RIGHT NOW!" Mr. Harris had arrived, followed by two vice-principals and some teachers. The fighters stopped, but Val remained on the ground, too stunned by the sudden violence to move.

"Now what happened here?" Mr. Harris demanded.

A Miramar kid nursing a bloody nose yelled, "It's the Winonas! They're always causing trouble."

"What's the matter, preppie? Scared?" a Winona guy sneered, and another fight almost erupted.

"All of you. In my office. NOW!" the principal ordered.

Val went to help Dirk. His hand covered one eye and the sleeve was ripped from his shirt.

"You all right?" she asked.

When he brushed his hair back, she saw his eye had started to puff and discolor. Val reached out but his bitter look made her freeze.

"I hope you're satisfied." He turned away from her.

"You can't believe I wanted this."

"No? Then why take the poll? And why publish it in the newspaper?" He struggled to his feet.

"I didn't," she protested. "I didn't know anything about it."

"Sure. Just like you didn't know anything about homecoming." He staggered slightly but she didn't dare offer to help.

Karen came rushing over. "Dirk, go to the nurse." She ignored Val. "Get something for your eye."

"Leave it." He sounded weary. "I'll be all right."

But Karen put her arm around him and led Dirk toward the nurse's office. Val wanted to be with him, to make him see it wasn't her fault, but Mr. Weymouth stopped her.

"Mr. Harris wants to see you. In his office."

"Now?" She had to talk to Dirk.

"Now." He looked grim.

Reluctantly, she followed him to the principal's office, wondering why he'd sent for her. Then she realized he probably wanted to know how the fight had started. Val would have preferred not being the one to tell him, but she had no choice.

When she entered his office, he ordered her to shut the door. She'd never seen him so angry.

"Sit down and tell me what went on out there." His hands gripped the edge of the desk as if he were maintaining control with an effort.

"One of the guys from Miramar made a crack about Winona. The Winona kid didn't like it, so—"

"So he used his fists." The principal's hand hit the desk, making Val jump. "Is this the way you settled things at Winona?"

She was appalled. "Of course not!"

He went on as if he hadn't heard. "Well, let me tell you, it's not the way we operate here. In the ten years I've been principal, I've never been closer to a full-scale riot than I was today. And I don't want it happening again. You hear me?"

He sounded like he blamed her. "I didn't start it!"

"No? What about your newspaper poll splitting the campus over some Christmas dance?" He waved an accusing finger at her. "Do you think that helped? Things have been explosive enough around here, and we've just managed to keep the lid on." His tone was threatening. "If you're going to actively stir up trouble—"

"I had nothing to do with that article in the paper," she protested.

"Then who did?" he demanded.

Val was stuck. She couldn't betray Nell.

Naturally, he interpreted her silence as guilt. "That's what I thought." Mr. Harris turned away as if he could not bear looking at her. "Ever since you've set foot on this campus you've done nothing but criticize Miramar traditions. I tried to be patient. Was even willing to give you your head on the rally schedule, let you turn homecoming into an air show, but was that enough? No!"

He was half out of his seat glaring at her now. "You've been nothing but a troublemaker in student council and I want it to stop. I will not have my campus divided. Do you understand?"

Shaken, Val whispered, "All I tried to do—"

"Was drive a wedge between council members, between Winona and Miramar kids." He sat back wearily. "Well, you've certainly succeeded. I hope you're proud of what you've done."

Val felt close to tears. Why did everyone blame her for splitting the campus? She had never wanted that to happen.

Somehow he had to listen to her. "Look, all I tried to do was give the campus some life, to bring along some ideas from Winona that I thought would work."

"By trying to ram them down our throats?" he challenged, his face set in angry lines. "And when that didn't work, you went behind Dirk's back and that of your advisor to get your own way. I'm surprised you even asked *my* permission."

Homecoming again. "All right, maybe I should have told Dirk," she admitted, "but every time I tried to suggest something different, no one would listen."

"Didn't that tell you anything?" He paused as if fighting for some semblance of control. "You can't force change. Our traditions go back twenty years, and we're proud of them."

"We were proud of ours at Winona too." Val knew she shouldn't argue but he had to understand.

"Winona's closed." The finality of his words reopened old wounds. "We're all sorry for your loss, but you have to put it behind you."

Didn't he think she'd tried? Stung, she retorted, "What you're saying is it's the Miramar way or nothing!"

"No! I'm not saying that at all!" The steel was back. "And if this is a sample of your attitude, no wonder the campus is in the mess it is today."

No one had ever spoken to her like that before. But whatever happened, she would not give him the satisfaction of seeing her cry. "Whether you believe me or not, I never wanted to cause trouble." Val cleared her throat. "I was only fighting for Winona's rights."

"No, you weren't." His words shocked her. "You were fighting for your own glory."

"That's not true—"

"You wanted to bring about changes all right, but not for Winona. For Val Robinson." He stood up. "But no school of mine will be sacrificed for someone's ego. You will either learn to work with Dirk and the student council, or I want your resignation. I will not put up with any more violence on my campus. Is that understood?"

Stunned, Val nodded and somehow got herself out of his office. She was shaking and needed to get away. The sixth period bell rang, and the passing kids looked at her curiously as she ran toward the parking lot.

Once inside the car, Val gripped the steering wheel for a moment, trying to stop the sobs before driving to the one place she could be alone—the beach.

On a rounded hill above the white sand spilling into the Pacific, she let go. Tears covered her face, but only the wind and the gulls were there to see. How could he say that about her? The article had been Nell's idea. But then, she wasn't entirely blameless either. If Val hadn't told her what Dirk had said, would Nell have thought of it?

Exhausted, Val blew her nose and stared at the ocean, her arms resting on her bent knees. Maybe she should have backed down, given in more. But what she wanted for the school wasn't wrong. She still believed that. Miramar was too stuffy, too stuck in tradition, and no matter what anyone said, they didn't want to include Winona ways. Someone had to fight for Winona's rights. But was that what she had been doing?

Val kicked off her shoes and dug her toes into the hot sand. Below her, two children fought over a beachball in the water. Suddenly, she was reminded of her and Dirk. As she watched the children struggle, she thought of the homecoming fight, the pep rally, and the Christmas dance. When the children lost the ball, she was not surprised, and watched their efforts to retrieve it. But each stroke pushed the ball beyond their grasp.

That was what had happened to her and Dirk. They had both wanted the ball, both wanted to keep their own school traditions, and had been unwilling to let go. Now, like the ball, campus unity was lost.

The tears started again and Val brushed them away impatiently. She needed to face the truth, however unpleasant. Was Mr. Harris right? Had her fight become a matter of pride, not principle?

Val didn't like to think so, but remembered her reaction to Dirk. He challenged her in some way that made her act with her emotions, not her mind. She'd called him stubborn, but she was just as bad. And pride had been at the source.

Mr. Harris had made her look at her motives, and she didn't like what she saw. The fact that Dirk was equally guilty didn't matter anymore. What was important was school unity, and to achieve that, Val knew she had to go back.

A look at her watch sent her scrambling to her feet, running barefoot over the sand to her car. When she arrived, the student council meeting had already started, but to Val's relief no vote had been taken. Nell and Tim were arguing as usual while Dirk tried to retain order.

"If you had your way, you'd be changing the school colors back to yellow and black," Tim accused.

Val noticed he was now wearing his Miramar jacket.

"Not a bad idea," Nell retorted before Dirk could intervene. "Better than that weedy blue and white."

"You're both out of order!" Dirk's eye was purple now, and she guessed the pain wasn't helping his temper. "Let's stick to the agenda. We're here to vote on the Christmas dance. Can we try to forget past differences and agree?"

"Sure we'll agree." Ray took the floor. "All you have to do is vote for the 'Holiday Hop.' "

Val could see nothing had changed. With the council split, the campus would continue the war. They needed to agree on the dance to show everyone that Winona and Miramar kids on the council could work together. That would have more effect than half a dozen orders from the principal.

Dirk made one last appeal. "Before we vote, keep in mind what happened this afternoon. The whole school is waiting for our decision. If we split, they do." He directed his words at Val. "But if we can agree on 'Winter Wonderland,' we ease the tension and show everyone we can work together."

He still couldn't back down. And why? Not because he believed in "Winter Wonderland" but to prove something to her. For both of them, giving in was a sign of weakness. It ought to be a sign of strength. She knew that now, and also knew what she had to do.

Dirk called for a show of hands. "Who wants 'Winter Wonderland'?"

As expected, all the Miramar kids raised their hands, but they had a majority. For Val had raised hers.

No one was more surprised than Dirk. And no one was more furious than Nell.

"Why did you do that?" she demanded as

soon as the meeting was over. Ray and Merrie were behind her, equally angry.

"You know why. It was best for the school." The day had drained Val, and all she wanted to go home.

But Nell was not through. "Which school? Miramar or Winona?"

"There's only one school now, Nell," Val said wearily. "Miramar, whether we like it or not."

"We don't!" Nell would not listen to reason. "And we don't like disloyal presidents either."

"She's gone on Dirk." Ray looked disgusted. "What can you expect?"

"That's not why I voted for 'Winter Wonderland'!" It had been hard enough to swallow her pride for the vote. She wasn't going to stand for their criticism too. "You know if we couldn't agree, it would only have caused more trouble on campus. Is that what you want?"

Nell ignored the question. "We wanted time. Time to get some of them on our side."

Why were they so blind? "Stop talking about sides," she yelled. "This isn't a war!"

"Maybe not for you, but it is for us." Nell's face had that determined expression Val had learned to dread. "We're not giving up yet."

"But what can we do?" Merrie stared at them helplessly.

"We use guerrilla warfare," Nell announced. "Okay, they wanted a 'Winter Wonderland,' they've got one. But suppose the posters don't get to the printers on time?"

Ray caught on at once. "And the band fails to show."

"We'll make them sorry they ever heard of 'Winter' or 'Wonderland,'" Nell gloated.

"No we won't!" Val put her foot down. "What kind of officers are you anyway?"

"Look who's talking? You're the turncoat. You're the one who voted against us," Nell taunted.

"Yes, I did, and I'm going to see to it that 'Winter Wonderland' is one of the best dances Miramar has ever seen. And if that means fighting every one of you, I will."

Val and Nell had squared off once before in junior high with Val the winner. Nell had never forgotten, which caused her to exclaim, "You really have gone over to the enemy, haven't you?" She looked close to tears. "Okay, you win. But I hope the Miramar kids appreciate what you've done. They'll be the only friends you'll have from now on."

They left Val standing alone in the council room, wishing she'd never heard of Miramar or "Winter Wonderland."

Chapter Twelve

The weeks before the Christmas dance were the longest Val had ever known. None of her Winona friends would speak to her, so she ate lunch alone, walked to classes by herself, and drove with the radio on for company. She missed Nell most of all.

Not that she had entirely forgiven her for the newspaper article, but before when they'd had a fight they'd always been able to talk out their differences. But when Val tried to call her, Nell wouldn't even come to the phone. That hurt. Couldn't Nell see that Val had had no choice? The violence on campus had shaken her into awareness and Mr. Harris' words had done the rest. Up to then, Val had never realized how easy it was to deceive yourself.

She'd been so quick to accuse Dirk of being stubborn, without ever backing down herself. Nor had she appreciated his attitude about homecoming. But when Nell had taken her unawares with that poll, Val realized why he'd been so upset. No one liked to be kept in the dark, especially by someone you trusted. Whatever the motives, the result was the same—a feeling of betrayal.

Even so, Val kept hoping maybe he'd call her.

But their only contact was at council meetings, and their conversation was strictly limited to school business. He remained polite but distant, and Karen followed his lead. Val left most of the preparation for the dance to him, unable to stand the sudden silences whenever she joined a group. Even the Miramar students didn't trust her, probably assuming she had some ulterior motive for voting their way. Val had never felt more alone.

Mr. Harris hadn't spoken to her again either, but she noticed he and all the administrators patrolled the campus daily during lunch hour. No more fights occurred, but the atmosphere remained tense. It was as if everyone were waiting for the next move. And the next move could come at the dance.

Dreading the evening, Val had delayed dressing until the last possible moment. Ralph was home for the weekend and found her staring into the mirror.

"Checking to see if you're the fairest of them all?" he inquired. The grind of graduate school had honed his body to further leanness, but although he looked tired, his eyes didn't miss a thing.

She made a face. "Whether I am or not doesn't matter. No one will notice anyway."

He walked to the windchimes and sent them whirling in a whisper of glass. "Self-pity's one way to handle it."

Her head jerked up. "You have a better idea?"

"Yeah! Face them down. Don't give them the satisfaction of knowing they got to you."

He was right. "Easy to say . . ."

"But hard to do? So are a lot of things." He wouldn't give her an inch. "Is Ray taking you?"

"No." Val smoothed the folds of her old white formal. "He and Merrie are a twosome now." And she was glad for them. Merrie's obvious adoration had put a swagger in Ray's step, but it didn't make her own isolation any easier.

Ralph picked up one of her Mexican pots, turning it absently in his hand. "What about Dirk?"

"He's probably taking Karen." She turned away to find her purse so she could hide her face and her hurt. "Anyway, didn't you know? I'm the school leper."

"Come here, leper." His hug was hard, brief, and brotherly, but very comforting. He looked at her. "So what about me? I'm free and wouldn't mind flexing the old feet."

She was touched but couldn't take him up on it. "Thanks anyway, but I have to do this alone."

"Proving something?" In many ways, they were quite alike.

She nodded. "To myself."

But when she arrived at the gym, Val was sorry she hadn't taken him up on his offer. Going in alone was harder than she'd ever imagined.

All she wanted to do was run, far from Miramar and Dirk and everyone, but she made herself walk inside. Everybody seemed to be watching her, and Val pretended interest in the clusters of snowflakes hanging from the ceiling. Never had she felt so naked, so exposed. Out of the corner of her eye, she saw Robyn nudge Tim.

Dirk was standing with Karen, and Val tried not to mind how radiant she looked in her silvery-green gown. When Dirk laughed at something she said, Val almost folded. Why did he always have to look so good? In dark maroon velvet, Dirk was the only Christmas present she really wanted. But no sense even thinking about him. It was all over between them, and that thought hurt most of all.

The kids paired off to dance, and feeling conspicuous, Val headed for the refreshment table. Trying to look like she was having fun, she tapped her foot to the music. Ray's brother's band had a good beat, but her eyes kept returning to Dirk. He was dancing with Karen, but Val was so preoccupied with her own pain that she didn't realize what was happening at first. Only when Dirk took the mike did she see the situation.

The dance floor had become a battleground. Hostile and uncooperative, the kids continued the campus feud, ignoring Dirk's efforts to make them mingle. When the Miramar couples were on the floor, the Winonas watched, muttering loud and rude comments. Val felt she'd strayed into a scene from *West Side Story*, and knew it was only a matter of time before a fight broke out.

Watching from the door, Mr. Harris looked tense, and Dirk seemed desperate. Perspiration covered his forehead and his eyes had a helpless look.

She went to him. No matter how he felt about her, she would always be there for him. He looked wary when he saw her approach.

"Can I try something?" she asked.

He hesitated, then handed her the mike. "Why not? I'm not doing much good."

Facing the kids was not easy, not after what had happened at the council meeting, but she had to do it.

Val cleared her throat. "Those of us on student council hoped you'd bury your differences and have a good time at the dance tonight."

"What about you?" Robyn yelled. "Are you ready to bury yours?"

Val swallowed but didn't flinch. "Yes. And I admit when I came here in September, I was big on change, critical of Miramar—"

"And you're not anymore," someone else yelled.

"I didn't say that." Val would not lie to them. She still felt Miramar had a long way to go to be the school of her choice, but now knew change would take time.

The next words were even harder. "But I see now that proving I'm right is no longer important. Getting you guys together is." Her hands began to tremble so hard she put them behind her. "Now how about meeting halfway—say on the dance floor? We'll have a friendship dance with a Miramar paired with a Winona student."

"You mean a war dance, don't you?"

Val couldn't see who spoke, so continued to plead with them all. "Come on, you guys. Just give it a try."

But when the music started, no one moved. She couldn't do any more and was turning away in defeat when Dirk came forward.

"May I have this dance?"

Val loved him so much at that moment, she could hardly speak. Blinking back the tears, she nodded.

Dirk led her onto the floor and the music changed to a slow, moody number. As she went into his arms, Val suddenly remembered their dance at homecoming. But this time their steps matched with neither trying to force the other.

Never had Val felt so in tune, so instinctively aware of each move Dirk made. They danced as one.

Over Dirk's shoulder she saw Nell watching, and knowing no one had joined them on the floor, Val sent her a plea for help.

Nell hesitated, then walked boldly over to Tim. Her voice carried clearly across the gym. "Want to dance?"

Val knew the risk Nell was taking, and held her breath. Taken by surprise, Tim could only stutter.

"Is that a yes?" Nell grinned.

He turned brick red as the kids began to laugh. In a moment, the two were on the floor. Soon Karen was paired with Ray, Robyn with Josh, until the gym was full of swaying, moving couples.

Dirk looked down at her. "I really admire what you did up there. It took guts."

"I was so scared they wouldn't go for it," she admitted, still not quite believing she was in his arms.

He glanced at the other couples. "This isn't the end of it though. You know that."

Val nodded. The Miramar–Winona conflict would not be solved by a friendship dance. "But it's a start."

"And you did it." His generosity made her denial even stronger.

"No, we did."

He held her even closer, as if trying to convey with his body what he couldn't say in words. She understood.

The band glided into another song, and Dirk

smiled down on her. "You know, I thought about calling you."

She thought of those hours waiting by the phone. "Why didn't you?"

"I don't know—pride, maybe. You really threw me when you voted for 'Winter Wonderland' though. I wanted to go after you even then but Tim said . . ." He hesitated.

"What did he say?" Val knew it was better if they got it all out in the open.

Dirk seemed to think so too. "He said you'd only changed your vote because of Mr. Harris. That he'd ordered you to."

"Tim was wrong. I made up my own mind. Not that Harris didn't start me thinking," she admitted.

Both glanced toward the door where the principal stood but now his face wore a genial smile.

Val continued, wanting Dirk to understand. "He said I wasn't fighting for Winona but for myself. Sort of an ego trip."

"He's crazy!" Dirk's defense made her feel good but she couldn't lie.

"That's what I thought until I started being honest with myself." Val moved closer within the circle of his arms. "Sure I wanted to bring some of Winona to Miramar, but soon it was more of a power struggle between you and me, one that split the whole campus."

She stopped, suddenly afraid he'd withdraw from her again, but she'd misjudged him. His eyes told her that.

More confident now, she confessed, "I took a good look at myself and didn't like what I saw. I wasn't fighting to help the Winonas but more to prove you were wrong."

"Sounds familiar." His laugh was rueful

"But I was so sure I was right."

"I know I was."

Val stiffened. Were they starting all that again? But his eyes were crinkling in that old teasing way. "Just like a politician," she sighed. "Never admits he's wrong."

"Oh I don't? We'll see about that." He propelled her quickly across the gym to the band platform.

"What are you going to do?" Val couldn't tell if he was serious or not.

"You're not the only one who can admit you're wrong" was all he would say before he took the mike. The music stopped and the kids faced him expectantly.

"Now that we're all friends again—"

"Looks like you and Val are more than that!" Tim yelled, and everyone laughed.

Dirk's arm only tightened more possessively around Val's waist and her attention was on Karen. She was smiling as she stood with Larry but Val recognized the pain in her eyes. She had cared for Dirk but had not come forward to claim or fight for him. Val would, but it seemed that wasn't Karen's way. She hoped Karen would find someone who would return her feelings, for she deserved the best.

Dirk was still speaking. "What I was trying to say before I was interrupted . . ." He pretended to glare at Tim. ". . . is we may have voted down Val's suggestion for a 'Holiday Hop,' but there's no reason we can't run a dance contest right here and now if you want it."

"WE WANT IT!" some kids shouted, and no one really objected.

More important, Val knew Dirk had understood what she'd been trying to say. He was showing her that now.

"We don't have a trophy for the winner, but we're good for it, right, Mr. Harris?" he called.

"The biggest we can find," the principal promised, and soon a teacher from Winona and one from Miramar were chosen as judges. Val found some construction paper left over from decorations and made contest numbers for each couple.

"Now choose your best dancing partner, and let's go!" Dirk turned to Val. "Ready, partner?"

She pinned on their number. "Ready."

The music moved from new wave to tango to disco to slow to rock. Val and Dirk managed to hang in till nearly the end, but were outclassed by Tim and Nell.

"I never knew you could dance like that," Val told her after they'd won.

"It's Tim." Her dimples appeared. "He brings out the best and worst in me."

"Mostly the worst." Val laughed, but Nell was suddenly serious.

"Can you forgive me? About the poll and all?"

"You were there when I needed you," Val said simply, and no more words were necessary.

Then Tim claimed Nell for the next dance, and Dirk couldn't resist ribbing him. "Change your mind about Nell?"

He didn't even blink. "Just doing my part for campus unity."

"I'll bet," Dirk scoffed as he took Val in his arms. "Do you think they'll bury the hatchet?" he asked.

"Hard to say." Tim and Nell were dancing

close but Val guessed from their quick verbal exchange that neither had conceded defeat.

She had one question. "Shouldn't you dance with Karen? I mean, if you brought her . . ."

"I didn't. Like you, I came stag."

That was all she needed to know. "Isn't it funny how we were always fighting, and look at us now." She snuggled closer.

"That's because you've learned to follow my lead." He sounded so smug, Val's head jerked up indignantly.

"Is that so?"

"Want me to prove it?" he challenged.

She stiffened. "You can try."

But when he told her what he had in mind, she did follow his lead. Right outside, where under the moon-streaked sky their lips met, and both forgot about fighting for a long, long time.

About the Author

Jo Stewart is the author of ANDREA, which won the Romance Writers of America's Golden Medallion Award for best published Young Adult romance of 1982, and BLUES FOR CASSANDRA. Both titles are available from New American Library's Signet Vista line. Ms. Stewart, who lives in California, is currently at work on a new romance for Magic Moments.

JOIN THE SIGNET VISTA READER'S PANEL

Help us bring you more of the books you like by filling out this survey and mailing it in today!

1. The title of the last paperback book I bought was:
   _____

2. Did someone recommend this book to you?
   (Check One) ☐ Yes ☐ No
   If YES, was it a ☐ Friend ☐ Teacher ☐ Librarian ☐ Parent.
   If NO, did you choose it because of: ☐ the cover ☐ the author
   ☐ the subject ☐ other: _____

3. Would you recommend this book to someone else?
   (Check One) ☐ Yes ☐ No

4. How many paperback books have you bought for your own
   reading enjoyment in the last six months?
   ☐ 1 to 3 ☐ 4 to 6 ☐ 7 to 10 ☐ 11 to 15 ☐ 16 or more

5. I usually buy my books at (Check One or more):
   ☐ Bookstore ☐ Drug Store ☐ Dept. Store ☐ Supermarket
   ☐ Discount Store ☐ School Bookstore ☐ School Bookclub
   ☐ School Book Fair ☐ Other:_____

6. Have you recently borrowed any paperback books from
   your: (Check One or More) ☐ Friends ☐ Parents
   ☐ Public Library ☐ School Library

7. What other paperback titles have you read in the last six
   months? Please list titles:_____
   _____
   _____

8. Who are your three favorite authors? _____
   _____
   _____

9. Do you read magazines regularly? (Check One) ☐ Yes ☐ No
   Please list your favorite magazines:_____
   _____

For our records, we need this information from all our Reader's
Panel members.
Name: _____
Address:_____Zip_____
Telephone: Area Code (   ) Number_____

10. Age (Check One): ☐ 10 to 11 ☐ 12 to 13 ☐ 14 to 15
    ☐ 16 to 17 ☐ 18 and over

11. Check One: ☐ Male ☐ Female

12. I am a: (Check One) ☐ Student ☐ Parent ☐ Librarian
    ☐ Teacher

13. I enjoy reading (Check One) ☐ Fiction ☐ Nonfiction books
    about (Check One or more): ☐ Friendships ☐ Romance
    ☐ Sports ☐ Humor ☐ Mystery/Adventure ☐ Science Fiction
    ☐ Teenage Problems ☐ Other:_____

Thank you for your help! Please mail this to the address listed
below.

NEW AMERICAN LIBRARY EDUCATION DEPARTMENT
1633 BROADWAY, NEW YORK, N.Y. 10019